nothing serious

nothing serious

TRANSLATED BY CHARLOTTE MANDELL

justine lévy

MELVILLE HOUSE PUBLISHING
HOBOKEN, NEW JERSEY

Translation © 2005 Melville House Publishing

Originally published in French as *Rien de grave*
© 2004 Editions Stock

Melville House Publishing
P.O. Box 3278
Hoboken, NJ 07030
mhpbooks.com

Book design: David Konopka

ISBN: 0-9761407-7-2

Printed in Canada

Library of Congress Cataloging-in-Publication Data
Lévy, Justine.
  [Rien de grave. English]
  Nothing serious / Justine Lévy ; translated by Charlotte Mandell.
    p. cm.
  ISBN 0-9761407-7-2 (pbk. original)
  I. Mandell, Charlotte. II. Title.
  PQ2672.E948R5413 2005
  843'.914—dc22

                                                    2005011936

nothing serious

justine lévy

one

I wore jeans to my grandmother's funeral. I didn't think it would shock people as much as it did; I thought no one would notice—she wouldn't have. My mind was on something else when I was getting dressed, I don't remember what, my grandmother isn't dead, they're not going to bury my grandmother, I have to call her up, that sort of thing.

Someone had organized a sort of party after the burial, party isn't quite the word, I don't know the right word for it, I took a taxi, I said to the man Go, but where? I don't know, maybe the Rue du Four, where my office is, and I escaped, I didn't want to go to this party, I've never liked parties, when I was young, thirteen or

.een years old, when I wasn't living with my father
my mother, I was living with her, my grandmother,
.e made me go out, go to parties at night, she lent me
dresses. There are grandmothers who make their grand-
daughters go to school or clean their plates; my grandmother made me go to parties.

But I have a pimple, I'd wail. That was the end of
the world for me, a pimple. I felt as if I were nothing
but a pimple, a giant pimple, What pimple, my grandmother would say without looking at me, where is it?
It's right there, on my nose, it's another nose on top of
my nose! No, dear, it's nothing, it's nothing at all, in
fact it's cute, we'll make it into a beauty spot. That's
okay, I'd say (a beauty spot on the nose, give me a
break) she got her way for the party, she made me up,
disguised me as her, or maybe as my mother, I don't
know, with coal-black eyes, cherry-red lips, glitter on
my eyelashes, it's true you couldn't see the pimple anymore. I was happy being someone else. I wasn't her,
not quite, but I was somebody else and I almost liked
myself, but I'd still cry in the car, I was so afraid and
so ashamed, the makeup wouldn't stay on, I couldn't
make the illusion last, Cinderella long before midnight,
I'd be silly and stupid and ugly and this time everyone
would realize it. The day of my grandmother's funeral,
in the taxi, I didn't cry. I'm not going to the party,

I said to myself. My grandmother is dead, I had the prettiest grandmother in the world but she is dead and I'm not crying.

My telephone rang, I remember. Private number, must be Adrien, or maybe Mom, always calling at the wrong time, always with bizarre emergencies, she's further west than me. Maybe she's crying, I said to myself. She loved her, she was her last link with Dad, maybe she's calling so we can cry together. But I didn't want that, I didn't want anything, nothing at all, just a cigarette, oh, but I was already smoking a cigarette, she'd leave a message in any case: Sweetie, Sweetie, are you there? Before, with Adrien, we'd often speak at the same time on the answering machine, a word each, or a sentence each, or else both of us saying the whole sentence at the same time, so happy we were to be together, happy and proud, two happy idiots proud of their true love, oh we'll show them, they'll see, we'll throw our great love in their faces, our insolent radiant love, this body with two heads, this soul with two bodies, or else he'd tickle me and make me laugh, or we'd say stupid things and our fathers would scold us, What kind of message is that, you aren't children anymore, that's not serious! Yes, it's serious, we seriously love each other, we haven't been children for a long time and we love each other super-seriously.

1-2-3, I see on my answering machine. It is Mom, then Dad, Gabriel, and then, in the saved messages, a message from her, my grandmother, her voice coming from so far away I can scarcely recognize it, Hello my little Lou, for her I was always her little Lou, it's her voice, there, in my ear, she is dead, but it's her voice, reassuring, enveloping, hello, hello, she called me from her little red telephone, she loved red so much, her red convertible, the red carpet in her bathroom, her red ski suit she lent me when I wanted to show off, it's her voice in my ear, everything is the same, the slight pause after Hello, the tinge of irony in My little Lou when she was so weak, already dying, and yet I don't cry. I don't cry but something in me stirs, a pinch at my heart, a throbbing like when you've run too fast, I shouldn't have listened to my answering machine I tell myself, but still I don't cry.

She told me Good riddance when Adrien left me. I'm broken into a thousand pieces, stunned, and she tells me Good riddance, he wasn't your type, he was a sleaze, a show-off. A show-off? A show-off of what? An empty show-off, someone who waves his arms around, is full of hot air, like that, that's what my grandmother said to me when the show-off left me. In the cemetery too I'm stunned, too shattered to cry, without any reaction, without any emotions, and in jeans, my grandmother loved jeans, she thought they showed off your ass nicely, she wore them all the time, she thought with nice shoes they could even be sort of chic. I'm wearing sort of hideous shoes so I'm not very chic, but what does it matter since she isn't there anymore to say to me, with her laughing, bright voice: Louise, how chic you look!

Not like Adrien, who pounces on me, leaping like a Mexican jumping-bean out of the packed, sniffling crowd, when we haven't seen each other for, what, six months, to choose that instant, that place, he could have warned me, he could have not come, he knows how I hate surprises. In any case I'm much too numb to be surprised, he pounces on me, his eyes red and his face all wrong, tense, sallow, with a funny twitch in his chin, like a tic, or a hiccup, he says Baby darling my little bear as he cries all over me, wringing his hands, his hands that are a little small, look at that, they're purplish at the knuckles, they're somebody else's hands. He's wearing a big watch, flashy, the kind worn by Important People and the people we used to make fun of, before, together, when we loved each other and when we were like Siamese twins who don't even need to explain why they make so much fun of other people, he's wearing an expensive watch that says I have a lot of money and not a lot of time but, look, I've come to your grandmother's funeral.

He looks pleased with his watch, pleased at being there and above all pleased at crying, pleased he can show everyone he's there and he's crying. Maybe he studied his new chin-twitch this morning, in the mirror. Maybe he tested it on Paula, the new woman in his life. The dreariness of a show-off, I tell myself as my grandmother would have said, letting him pull me towards him. And then when he detaches himself (I don't respond to his embrace, I let my arms dangle on either side of his jacket, Does the jacket look okay? He must have asked Paula before he went out) I feel my neck all wet from his tears, yuck. He looks hard at me, looks me up and down, with a mixture of disbelief and disapproval: my jeans, of course.

I am not sad that day. My grandmother is dead, but I'm so swollen inside, so desperate, so destroyed, that I'm not sad, and I don't cry. Around me, tons of people I don't know, people crammed together and bathed in tears, people who look like they know why they're there and why they're sad, people who must have come from far away, from Marseille, from Madrid, from Tel Aviv, from New York, they are her relatives, my relatives, they loved her, they also seem to love me too, so sorry, please accept my condolences, if I can do something, she was so unique, don't hesitate to call. And my father, his sadness, I had never seen my father as sad as that, I had never understood that my father was also a son, but why is he crying like that? Is it because he's noticed that his daughter, next to him, is not crying? Or is he crying too much because he's noticed that I can't manage to cry? They're all crying. And they all come towards me. And tell me nice things or awkward things or tender things. And all I can think is shut up, shut up already, I'm not crying why are you, and I keep my head lowered, I doodle in the dirt with the tip of my sneaker, circles, hearts, squares, I just feel guilty at being there and not crying, guilty I'm in jeans, guilty for being ditched by a sleaze and for being alive and for being in jeans and for not crying. I think dead, dead, dead, she is dead, departed, deceased, she's kicked the bucket, dead, dead, dead, and it has no effect on me. This fucking life. One dumb love affair gone wrong and all of a sudden you become a little dry-hearted bitch who looks nastily at kind people and who can't even be bothered to cry at her own grandmother's funeral.

I cry easily, usually. I cry for anything. When I fall down, when I have a toothache, when someone bumps

into me, when I'm afraid, when I'm tired, when I want
to be left alone, there, that's what I'd really like, for people to leave me alone and for my cell phone to stop ring-
ing. They must be wondering what I'm doing. No one
saw her after the cemetery? She was so sad, poor little
Louise. She must have run off to hide and cry in peace.

When was the last time I cried? When I ordered
steak tartare, at the café near my place, and realized I
hadn't brought any money with me, and instead of saying anything I ran out the door and since then I've had
to make ridiculous detours to go home? When I drew
a moustache on a life-sized Paula behind a bus shelter
and an old lady treated me like a juvenile delinquent?
When I wanted to take off my wedding ring and my
finger began to swell up and I had to have it cut off?
No. I didn't cry then either. Dumped, left, jilted, shock
has chernobylized me. And that's probably why I snuck
out of the bistro and made my finger swell up on
purpose: to cry, to feel the need to cry, good warm
reassuring tears, the good consolation of flowing tears.

My grandmother is dead. Today I'd like to feel even
a tiny desire to cry, a tiny wish to believe it's true, but
it's no use—I've lost tears the way other people lose
their sight or speech.

two

Mom's little bald head, in the gap of my bedroom door, this morning, on the Rue Bonaparte. The pruritus covering her arm. Her other arm, which has grown to twice its size, which she is massaging with careful, conscientious movements, as she contentedly watches Pablo and me wake up. I want some La Prairie skin cream, she said to me the other day, they make the best in the world. So I ordered her some creams from La Prairie, on the internet, with her ex's credit card. Cream with extracts of caviar, cream with an exclusive energizing complex, cream with vitamin C with fresh sheep placenta cells with 3-alpha-hydroxy-acids. They're super, sweetie-pie, super, she said. But the days went by, she didn't mention them to me anymore and one day when I was rummaging around in her toilet kit to see if she'd used them or passed them on to a girl-friend, I saw that the tubes were intact. She had just underlined some warnings on the flyer in red: "If irri-tations appear, consult your doctor." She had written things in the margins: "Warning! Warning, face-lift!" On another leaflet, which came with a free sample, she had drawn a box around "a unique combination of vegetable extracts to balance the complexion" and "glowing, firm skin, a new youth." She sure isn't mas-saging herself with a La Prairie cream, as she stands at my bedroom door. It's some kind of cheap ointment that smells like the hospital and, even at this distance, makes me nauseous.

My mother—enormous, swollen—just has one breast now, but she's happy to be there and wake us up. On her left side, where there's nothing, just the enormous scar, she has folded over a scarf I brought her back from Formentera. Her purple straw hat is too loose, it almost comes down over her ears, but I gave it to her so she wears it all the time, starting in the morning, like this morning. It's not as hot as the wig, she says, and you can even use it to wipe the sweat off your forehead when you perspire. You see, sweetie-pie, cancer is just a question of organization, in the end. Okay, Mom, okay. But still when you're so sick how can you seem so happy?

She gets up every other hour at night, to pee. Once her plan has been formed—not formed, but precipitated—she tries not to make any noise but that's worse, or else she makes noise on purpose to warn us, watch out, I'm here, it's me, don't be indecently naked it's me, Alice. She tries to go quickly, she takes big steps that frighten my cats, not her own cat who follows her meowing and wakes up Pablo: What's happening, what's happening, it's nothing, it's Mom, go back to sleep. She drinks quarts of Tuocha tea, she pronounces it *tuyau de chat*, "cat tube," tea with lemon juice in the morning on an empty stomach, since it's good for her liver. Her screwed-up liver, swollen from metastasis. I keep wanting to tell her I'm sorry. But sorry for what? For not helping her more. Or helping her so badly, on and off, the way I usually do things. A day when we're present to each other, with lots of gifts, window-shopping, long conversations, makes me happy, and her too. And then the next day my egoism gets the upper hand, and my cowardliness, and my wish, ever since Adrien left me, to run away from unhappiness, all unhappiness, even my so-sick mother's: You have to be extremely happy in order to bear being sad, extremely happy or extremely brave, and I'm not very brave, and I'm very very unhappy.

So I'm present in fits and starts. I send her text messages. I go with her every five weeks for her chemo sessions. I buy her salmon caviar which she eats with a teaspoon and organic hamburgers; the homeopath said a pound of red meat per day, 500 grams, to make the platelet count go up. I go with her to the masseuse who reduces the swelling in her arm. And then I go back to my office, and I go on foot to pick her up afterwards. It's too close to take a taxi, but it's too far for her, so tired, she must at all cost avoid a dizzy spell, so we hobble along, both of us, me supporting her, her limping a little, with all the nasty people in the neighborhood looking away so they don't have to greet us—I, her own daughter, am afraid of the sight of adversity, so what must it be for a stranger....

But I think I'm being misleading. I think she thinks I take good care of her. On the whole, I take care of her the way she used to take care of me, every-other-weekend-and-half-vacation-time. Except she was amazing, when Adrien left. There all the time, making me laugh, cooking for me, waking me up in the morning, she was never so present as she was then, it was so miraculous, so new, that I even had the impression, at times, of not feeling any more pain. I'm not like that. Even when I'm there, I'm much much worse than Mom. For instance I pretend at night that I have a lot of work to do and she pretends to believe me. Actually, before I go home, I dash off to the pool, my little well-being, my little muscles, she must sense it, she knows me, and then she must sniff the chlorine when I kiss her. And my terror at finding myself alone with her, after her chemo sessions, when she is delirious: She's feverish, crying, laughing, asking forgiveness, she's very cold, very hot, she says whatever comes into her head and, even if I know she was never very conventional, even if I pretend nothing's the matter, still I'm petrified and I just want to run away.

When I sense that she's less determined, less certain of getting better, or even wanting to get better or accepting the treatment that's destroying her, on the vomiting days, the days when she can't do anything but vomit, when she can't bear it any more, when I sense that the wish to stop suffering is stronger than the wish to live, I get her onto the subject of Adrien. That gets on her nerves right away, that puts her right back on her feet, upsy daisy she's off, that-bastard-and-his-witch-that-perverse-incestuous-couple, oh those vulgar awful people, she detests them, she'll take over now, from me and from my grandmother, she wants to write to him, to break his neck, suddenly she's hungry, she has tremendous energy, she's going to get better and give him a thrashing. Once she's gotten started I'm happy for a few hours, or a few days, I can leave her alone, I know she's going to be active, see friends, take her medication, build up her plans for revenge, curse. And then that's all used up and something else has to be found. I don't always find it, I'm a little tired, of her, of me, of her sickness, of the long evenings when she talks all the time, when she can't stop talking, intelligent funny things, and then boring things, especially when I don't feel like talking, or when I want to watch TV, she always has something to say whenever you have to concentrate.

Pablo is there, he is polite to her, he was well brought-up, she is my mother after all, I think he finds her eccentric, but she talks to him all the time, she wants to be useful to him too, she clips newspaper articles for him that he's already read, she buys a subscription for him to the SOS Plumbers hotline that it takes him three months to cancel, she comes into our bedroom, like this morning, with tea, quick, quick, pull up the comforter, too late, she saw him naked, she says that's okay that's okay, it's time to get up, here's some tea with honey, it's good for what ails you, he mumbles thanks, her feet get caught in the clothes we've thrown on the floor and the tray falls out of her hands and the tea scalds us.

Later on, when I'm wide awake, I'll say to her Mom I don't want you to come into my bedroom like that in the morning, I'm not alone, I'm not fifteen anymore. She'll realize this, she'll be humiliated, she'll be mortified, she'll be ashamed, she'll want to go back to her place, she'll vomit all night. But I too will be ashamed, what difference can it make, who cares if she comes into my room, she's sick, she wants to catch up on all those years without honeyed tea, sure, she's violating our privacy a little, but what privacy, what the fuck do I care about my privacy, she is so, she is so, what words are there for that kind of tenderness, that love, I don't have the right words anymore, you need words that don't exist, sometimes I want to take her cancer from her, steal it away from her, but is that to ease her pain or is it out of jealousy, to be made a fuss of in her place? I hate myself for thinking that. I hate the stone heart I've become.

I hate her cat too. I'm her cat, and it's her cat that sleeps with her, she takes such good care of it, the veterinarians, the treats, the caresses, and me too, Kitten, Kitten, that's what she calls me, she calls me Kitten when she yells at me, Kitten when she kisses me, Kitten for everything, it's a matter of intonation, I am her cat, her real cat, a cat that doesn't cry at its grandmother's burial, a cat that always dresses the same way, a cat that doesn't answer the telephone, a cat that doesn't like parties, a cat that sleeps all the time, that likes to be left alone, I'm her cat, so why does she keep talking to the other one, the cat cat, the other stupid cat, why does he piss on my things and emit monstrous cries at night, almost human cries? I say to her Mom, couldn't you leave your cat at your place sometimes, or at a friend's place, that'd give us a little time off, he keeps me from sleeping, plus he has fleas, plus he's not happy here, he doesn't feel at home, you know a cat is more attached to his territory than to his owner, what do you have to do with this cat, you think you love him but it's not true, he doesn't even have a name, he's sick, he's hideous, he's always in our way, I hate him.

She replies Yes yes Kitten. She says she understands, she's going to get organized, she's better off at her place anyway. And she goes back to Montmartre, with her cat, and she sulks, and she doesn't come back. But Mom, that's stupid, I was stupid, please forgive me, come back, come back with him, jealous of a beast how beastly, come back I'll wear earplugs. But she's upset, she has her stubborn look, she'll stay for days, for weeks, without returning to Rue Bonaparte. I wasn't so mean, before. That's what Pablo says: Maybe this whole affair has messed me up.

three

I'm neglecting Mom too much. I think about her all the time, I don't even need to think about her to think about her, she's always with me, like a weight, a regret, a gentle presence, a huge despair, but I'm neglecting her.

Even today, when I'm feeling better, when Adrien is far away and I'm glad he's far away, even today when I have lots of time, beautiful dry spring day, movies with Pablo, pretended indifference, laughter, I realize that I'm thinking of her, but not enough, I should be doing more, much more, but what? I'm not really sure but I know it, I'm convinced she needs me so she can get better, and it upsets me that I'm not there for her.

The other day, we were on the terrace of the Pré aux Clercs, she was shivering, had hot flashes, drops of sweat drenching her scarf, I had gotten her onto Adrien to get her a little worked up, and a girl passed by, magnificent, provocative, beautiful enormous breasts in a tight T-shirt, people were turning around, I said Mom did you see her tits! She smiled. But, before the smile, a shadow passed and I wanted to slap myself because this shadow meant: I used to have beautiful breasts too, before, I was proud of my breasts, even when they photographed them, even when you saw nothing but them on the cover of *Vogue*, on the beach, on the café terraces, they used to say Alice's breasts, Alice and her breasts, there are some girls who even when they're dressed always seem naked, I was one of those girls. And then the girl was gone, and it was over, and Mom smiled: I wanted to hold her in my arms, to tell her they'll make you a brand new one, a new breast, you'll be very beautiful, like before, you'll see; but it was too late, she wouldn't have understood, she had already started off on Adrien.

I remember the day she told me she was sick. She came unannounced to my office. I can see her approaching in the hallway, we can all see her, her quick step, her regal bearing, her features a little drawn, maybe, but not too much, and she looks good that way anyway, with her everything looks good, as soon as she gets out of bed she's beautiful, dead drunk she's beautiful, unhappy she's beautiful, everything agrees with her, fatigue and love, exultation and languor, my mother is a miracle, my mother makes heads turn, my mother in a miniskirt always causes a pile-up, she's walking down the corridor, her little hippie straw bag, her yellow capris, kimono, she's out of breath, as always she has something urgent and serious to tell me, as always she's going to get muddled up, go off on digressions and diversions, I feel it 50 feet away, just seeing her appear, just seeing that concentrated look she has now that moves me or annoys me depending on the day, from 50 feet away I can tell that she's coming once again to dish up one of those absurd mixed-up stories whose secret she holds.

I'm in my office, then. I'm bored. It's hot. I overdid it a little on the Xanax and the marijuana so as not to think about Adrien and to be able to go to work. Dad bombarded me with telephone calls until I woke up and today he told me You are going to go to work, that's an order, so I obeyed and here I am, useless and adrift, in the middle of all these manuscripts, all these future non-books almost as useless as me, which, just thinking about them, already make me want to yawn with boredom. I'm happy to see her. I'll play the game, hear her story out, take seriously her exaggerations, her difficulties, her unlikelihoods, sometimes it's just a matter of small change, her bag was snatched in the subway, or the bastards at the Post Office are on strike, or she was paid in forged currency, or she has to help out a close friend, yes of course you know her, you know her very well, it's Françoise, she used to look after you when you were little, she took care of you when you had chickenpox, she saved you from drowning, she wrote an article on your father, well she's in jail because of a misunderstanding, she needs 1,546 Francs and she doesn't have it, the ATM outside my place ate up my Visa card. Usually I call Dad, I fix up the story or make it plausible or invent another one, Dad doesn't have time to be suspicious, he has something else to do, or else he really believes us: In any case it doesn't matter, if Mom says she needs money, with her so proud, so egotistical, with her cock-and-bull stories, he knows this is her last recourse, she's used up all the other ones and you have to pretend to believe her. She charges towards me. I'm ready. I go close the door. We'll have a little tea in the office. She'll talk, talk, tell me her super-complicated story and we'll find a solution, we always find a solution.

The first thing that strikes me, actually, isn't really her capris, her tense features, her basket; it's her long hennaed hair spilling out over her shoulders. A few months ago, on the phone, she told me she was going to have it cut, so it could grow back stronger. I wasn't happy. I don't like change. It frightens me when people change, especially Mom, and especially her hair, that's the first image that comes to me when I think of her, her long silky red hair, reaching down to her waist: When I was little, we sometimes spent months and months without seeing each other, months are endless when you're little, they're twice as long, or three times, or more, but she had given me a lock of her hair for those times, and I still have it with me, this lock, it's very long, very soft, it smells, even today, of the same mixture of honey shampoo, old-fashioned perfume and Virginia tobacco. Today her hair is very beautiful, very shiny, like nylon, and it's not just the first thing I see, but the first thing I say to her when she comes into my office: Oh, Mom, how nice your hair looks! And, without looking at me, taking her time sitting down opposite me, lighting a cigarette, getting a handkerchief out of her basket and wiping off the sweat that's forming a sheen on her forehead: "It's not my hair, Kitten."

Suddenly, I don't understand. I tell myself she's saying any old thing, it's a farce, a prank, a wig for when she acts in a movie, a word game I haven't grasped the meaning of yet. I say:

"What do you mean, not your hair?"

"No, kitty, it's not my hair."

This tone of voice, this seriousness, this bitterness that is so unlike her, this look of defeat, this half-open mouth, this fixed stare, suddenly it doesn't seem at all like a farce. The rest I hear in a fog, one word out of two, sentences that don't make sense and seem to come from miles away before reaching me, my head empty, my heart pounding.

"...your father... cancer... didn't want me to talk to you about it... your grandmother's death... Adrien... wanted me to get better first and tell you after... but it's going to take a long time, my little Kitten... longer than he thinks... he'll be furious... furious... he says it's to protect you... but I think that's worse... I think that to cure cancer, cancer, cancer..."

"But what are you talking about?" I shout. "What's all this stuff about cancer?"

And I pounce on her. And, without thinking, like a Fury, I pull at her beautiful silky hair and it comes off in my hand, all of it, and her little round skull is beneath.

Sit back down, the soft dead thing left on the table between us. Raise your head. Shiver. Look at the ceiling. Don't cry, above all don't cry, she needs me, Mom needs me I tell myself, don't cry, be strong.

"Give me a cigarette," I mutter, praying the tears don't come.

Concentrating, knitting her brows, she rummages in her basket and holds out her pack of Benson & Hedges Light, BHL's, Adrięn used to say, your mother smokes BHL's, and that annoyed him, since they're my father's initials.

"Are you angry at me?"

"For what, Mom?"

"For telling you, for disobeying."

I wanted to reply are you crazy or what? Be angry at you? At you? That would be the last straw! I'm made of sterner stuff than that! What do you people think? We're stronger, the two of us, three of us with Dad, you have to stop treating me like a baby! But I'm too scared of breaking down in tears, of not being able to finish, of losing my footing, so I just say no, no, it's better like this, and I let myself take in this new piece of information, which I can scarcely formulate it seems so sacrilegious to me: cancer... chemo... Mom has cancer and chemo has already made her hair fall out... how could I not have noticed anything? Not have guessed anything? What sort of monster am I for not feeling anything? Why her? How is it possible for it to happen to her? Wasn't she unsinkable? Immortal? Hasn't she survived one or two overdoses, suicide attempts, grief, madness?

Timidly, like a thief, as if she were taking advantage of my looking away, she retrieves her wig from the table, her crumpled wig, and puts it back on her head. It's not bad, that wig, I realize. It's a perfect imitation of her old hairstyle. Except Mom doesn't have a mirror and she puts it on the wrong way, too low on the forehead, spilling over on one side, and suddenly it makes her look like a little clown. And then a completely unplanned and very stupid thing happens: Instead of talking, I laugh, and my mother, surprised at first, then reassured, her eyes full of the tears I've managed to hide, bursts out laughing too. We laugh together, for a long time, like two idiots, like two madwomen, we laugh heartily, a healing laugh that washes away all the pain we had in talking to each other about this great sorrow we're beginning to share.

Our tour of all the doctors started that day. Waiting rooms. Consultations. The hope, each time, that one of them will invalidate the diagnosis, but you're not sick, you don't have cancer, the same way, when I was five, I went with Dad to five different ophthalmologists to make sure I really needed glasses. Never in my life have I been spending so much time with her. And it won't always be easy because she'll take advantage of it to get involved in everything. My life. Adrien. My lovers who help me survive Adrien.

My three lovers or pseudo-lovers at the time, she'll become completely infatuated with them, she'll break out into tears when I leave them, she'll call them or arrange to meet them by chance and tell them don't do anything, Louise will come back, she's a little upset right now but she'll come back. And I of course will get angry and immediately afterwards will hate myself for getting angry.

I understood, after a while, that Mom was stronger than I thought, braver, more courageous, and just thinking about her, just seeing her, all unsteady but smiling and putting on lipstick after emerging from her fortnightly chemo, I have, even today, tears in my eyes. But I'm the one that's falling apart. I'm the one spending days cursing, getting into black rages, damning the entire planet for all the unhappiness that's falling on my head. Unfair, that Mom is sick. Unfair, that the doctors can't cure her right away: So what good are they? What good are they? Unfair that Mom found out about it so late, stage three, in a scale from one to four, how could she not have seen it coming? Unfair, the charlatans who, early on, swung a pendulum in front of her breast and murmured no chemo, chemo's like the atomic bomb, you'll be able to cure it with thyme herb tea. Unfair, that Mom believed them, and unfair, that I, Louise, believed them too, a little, for five minutes, afterwards I bawled her out, why did we go consult that moron? But it didn't do any good to bawl her out, Mom has also passed the age when you can be bawled out. Mom and I have a complicated history. I'm even more moronic than Mom, when it comes down to it. And unfair, finally, Adrien, unfair, that evil Adrien who chose just that instant, on purpose, to ditch me...

I make him responsible for everything. My sadness is him. My nightmares, him. My bulimia and my anorexia, the death of my grandmother and the assassination of Commander Massoud, the bad weather, SARS, the Israeli-Palestinian conflict, my first wrinkle, my crows feet, it's all still him. Mom's sickness, too! How could I not make him responsible for my mother's sickness? He planned it all, I tell myself. Premeditated everything. He could have helped me, if he'd stayed. His mother, his sisters, his brother, his grandmother, his father, his entire family, they'd all have set themselves to the task, there'd have been lots of us to comfort Mom. Instead of that, his idiotic phone messages, his plaintive voice, his boorish bastard's text messages, Paula, my new life, I'm happy as a king, why won't you call me back? And he's guilty for that too. It does me good to think that.

Sadness plus sadness, I don't know if that makes twice as much or half as much sadness. From a certain point of view, it's twice. You tell yourself: what next? What else is going to land on my head? Is there a limit to grief? But it's true that at the same time looking after Mom kept me busy, it let me put a name on a suffering that didn't have one, I had a valid reason to be unhappy and I used this sorrow to ease the other one, I used Mom's sickness to lighten a lousy love affair. I curse myself for saying that. I curse myself for thinking it. I hate myself.

four

I've just met Pablo. He's sitting on the sofa, legs crossed, beautiful teeth, beautiful face, he's talking to me about some film about Manolete, or Enrique Ponce I'm not sure, and about matadors, life, death, the bull's horns, he wants so much to impress me, he'd be so happy if we could at least share that, him and me. So sometimes I pretend a little, I pick up the first nice sentence that's left unfinished and dangle it in front of him as you would with a cat, I wouldn't dare say as with a dog, that's too violent, I'd rather it be with a cat. But still, I don't want to pretend or ask questions or go into raptures, oh yes great let's go to Seville, let's go to Nîmes, I don't want to offer him or owe him that,

I don't want to cede anything, don't want to give in on anything, I know that actually, if I let myself go a little, he'll end up fascinating me, but I don't want anything to fascinate me, nothing.

I like Pablo. He's not my type. He isn't at all like me. But that's just what I like. The Siamese Twin stage, the two-headed eagle, sharing the same brain, slipping into someone else's life as you would into warm clothing, all that infantile garbage, that's over. Sometimes I just want Pablo to shut up, or go away.

"What do you want to do, then," he asks me, seeing me walled up in my foul mood, "what do you want to do with your life?"

I don't want anything, that day, not to listen to him and not to not listen to him, not to be quiet and not to be not quiet, maybe just to stay there and smoke a cigarette, in any case I don't want to know what life is going to be like and how I see the future, because we always come to that point with him and now it makes me want to vomit, no, go to sleep.

"Nothing," I reply clenching my teeth, looking towards the fuzzy form on the sofa. (I didn't put on my contacts. To annoy him even more, I decided to play the mean little blind girl who can't see beyond the edge of her bed.)

"But what interests you in life?"

"Nothing."

"Oh good. You want to do nothing."

"No."

"Do you want to be a mother? Do you want to have children?"

"Nah."

"Okay. Great.... You want to be passive, right?"

"Yes."

"Let yourself go with the flow."

"Yeah."

"You want to be a houseplant, a bathing suit, you want to be Mouna Ayoub."

"I want to be left alone," I shout.

He doesn't say anything. He never gives up. We've known each other for just a few weeks, but he's read the manual, he knows it always blows over, after a while I'll be back to normal, almost nice, he just has to wait, arch his back, or maybe not, maybe he hasn't read the manual, I'm confusing him with Adrien. Had Adrien read the manual? Or was it a complete misunderstanding from the beginning? Was the whole story already written from the very first argument, when I was jealous, already, of one of his new stepmothers and he said I was crazy? And right in the middle of the crisis he suddenly asked me, as if it was the only thing that counted: Do you have a hairbrush?

Pablo doesn't say anything, he gets up from the sofa and begins to walk back and forth in the big empty living room. The first time he came to my place he said wow it's empty, there's nothing here, with an alarmed look. Also with the look, at the same time, of someone who wanted to set things right. I was surprised, almost annoyed, it's true it was a little empty, but I didn't think there was nothing. I liked it when he brought his things over right away, his posters of bullrings, his books, piles of CD's, jumbled together, singers I didn't know, he turns up the volume, that doesn't bother me, the only thing I don't want is for him to ask me to get involved, to love, to appreciate, to feel the difference, no, that I do not want, but he doesn't ask it of me, he's too afraid of my foul mood to ask me to be nice. Right away he messed everything up with his stuff, his own life, and that too I liked, the impression when I came home that something's underway, that this space I didn't know how to fill, this hole-like space, was occupied by Pablo and his pigsty. So he starts pacing in the not-so-empty living room. I'm just beginning by now to get used to his walk. It becomes superimposed onto Adrien's. Between his footsteps, Adrien's can be heard less and less, as if he were crushing him by walking, as if Adrien were disappearing under the earth thanks to Pablo. He comes up to me, takes my cigarette to light his own, breathes in the smoke through his nose like a bull ready to charge and says in a very gentle voice: "No, I won't leave you alone."

Good grief, what a nutcase, I think. Doesn't he understand you don't argue with a girl who doesn't give a damn about anything and who could explode at any instant?

"So I'll leave you," I reply.

"What?"

"I'll leave you. I'll leave you. I'll leave you."

"You're crazy, Louise, you're crazy."

"Go away."

"No, I won't go away. I won't leave you in this state."

"What state, this isn't a state, it's how I am, I want to be alone, don't you understand? Alone, alone, alone, alone, alone!"

"To do what, then?"

"Nothing! To do nothing, nothing at all!"

"Then write! Or make a collage, a movie, a song, do something with all that, at least it'll have been some use."

"You're driving me crazy with your enthusiasm, you always see the good side of things, I don't have a good side, that's what you can't seem to grasp, I want to be alone, to wait for nothing, hope for nothing, sleep smoke eat hibernate, not to think, not to reflect, clean the floor with a Swiffer WetJet, play Super Mario World

on my computer, read old *Elle* magazines, old copies of
20 Ans, novels I know by heart, keep underlining the
same sentences, watch TV, drink milk, eat bread
dipped in tea, and dance, dance all by myself because
I can't in front of others, it's like an orgy, it's disgusting, not to cry, not to laugh, to get massaged, to be
caressed, without reciprocating, inert, as inert as possible under the fingers of the masseuse who I pay for this
luxury, snore, fall asleep!"

"That's it. Like your cats, right? Great."

"Yes, great, I'm a cat, great! Didn't I already tell you
my mother used to tie me to a leash? That was the
fashion, a rope around your waist, she pulled it
towards her to cross the street, it shocked all the bourgeois people, she dressed me in black, people insulted
her, it was great."

"Stop, Louise, you're not funny now."

"I know I'm not funny, I'm leaving you."

"No, you're not leaving me."

"Yes I am."

"No. I love you."

"It's stupid to say that, that's the stupidest sentence
in the world. I don't love you, I'll never love you, I'll
never love anyone."

"Adrien messed you up."

"That has nothing to do with you."

"Yes it does. Because I love you."

"No you don't, I don't want you to love me, my heart is all dried up, it's stale."

"I'll water your heart. I'll water it, you'll see. Come, come close to me, there, look...."

"I used to be amazing, before. But now, now, now..."

"Now what?"

"Now I'm ruining you."

"He's the one who ruined you. You'll love me, you'll see."

"I'm tired."

"No you're not."

"Say something nice to me...."

"I'm saying it."

"Thank you, thank you, I can't bear any more."

That's how we didn't leave each other. It's been two years now. He knows he can't ask anything of me. He doesn't know a lot about me, but he knows that, I have nothing to give him, and I don't expect anything of him. Maybe that makes him suffer. Maybe he's waiting, maybe he thinks he'll cure me. At the time, after the argument, I completely forbade any sweet-talk. How obscene sweet-talk is, worn out and overused, I think it's dishonorable to say I love you to a woman, I think that should be grounds for a separation between a man and a woman, I forbid us to use words, I want to make sure that feelings won't follow them so one morning we'll wake up with love that's fled, like that, bingo, just the way it came.

Pablo is kind. He pretends to understand. No more love? He says. No more sweet-talk? Still there's all the rest and the rest is immense, beginning with syllables, the color of the voice, intonation. And it's true that when he says Louise to me on the phone, do you understand Louise, can you hear me Louise, when he talks to me at night with his way of rounding out his lips, Lou like a caress, or a moue, and his way when he says -eez of detaching the syllable and showing his chalk-white teeth that don't reflect light but absorb it, when he says Louise like that, I have nothing to reproach him for since he hasn't said anything, and he hasn't uttered the big forbidden words, but it's like a stolen caress, and I like it. It's cheating a little, true. But it's okay. I can't get angry. Anyway I don't get angry. It's good, just my first name. It's almost tender. He whispers my first name and it's like the sweetness of things coming back to me.

five

Nobody at my office on the Rue du Four. That's normal,
it's lunchtime. Sit down. Think. Go over the whole story
from the beginning, how, why. Paula's arrival at
Porquerolles with Adrien's father, her cheerfulness, her
liveliness, she called him the man of my life, they seemed
to love each other and laugh a lot together, she made me
laugh too in the beginning. When did I realize she wanted the son after the father and she was pretending to be
cheerful but she just wanted to destroy, to create the
maximum amount of tragedy and unhappiness? This
annoying noise in my head, which keeps me from thinking right. Open the window, but there's almost as much
noise outside. Close the window, bang, that makes even

more noise, like a sudden impact in the void. Massage my temples, maybe? Massage the roots of my hair? Before Mom used to do that. No one in the world knows as well as Mom does how to put gloomy thoughts to rest. But these aren't gloomy thoughts, they aren't even thoughts at all, it's just noise in emptiness, and Mom is so sick, it's my turn now to give her massages. No one will ever massage me the way Mom did. No one. No thoughts, no feelings, nothing, I think I've thrown everything away.

The wedding photos—I was wearing too much makeup anyway—thrown away.

Your letters, the letters where you said, no, stop remembering what you said to me in your letters, thrown away.

Thrown away the absurd, poetic collages we gave each other when we were in love and children and dead-broke.

Thrown away my wedding ring, or rather the cut-up pieces of my wedding ring, my ring finger swollen, just a little psychosomatic symptom, you're sure you don't want to keep the pieces the lady at the jewelry store asked me, no thanks, keep everything.

And then that manuscript, there, on my shelf, put there by chance: A horrible manuscript, it'd make you

vomit, puke, everything makes you want to puke, in
any case, the rejection letter to come will make you
want to puke, the hope of the guy at the other end
waiting for the letter makes you want to puke, throw
it out too, get rid of it, that would be better for everyone, for him, for me, for the publisher, for the editors,
throw the whole stack out while you're at it, go on,
throw out this one, that one, fill a big trashbag, bound
manuscripts, already rejected by other publishers that's
obvious, they tried to tear off the label but it shows,
hardbound covers, pathetic illustrations, little cover letters, all those efforts, those schemes, out you go, throw
it all out, talent, mediocrity, dazzling writing, throw
that out too, annihilate, cram it into the wastepaper
basket, drag it into the hallway, put it in front of the
door, go get another bag, fill it up, there are lots of
manuscripts, way too many, they're all crap, go on, out
with you, books too, there's too much published everyone's saying so, clean everything out, spring-cleaning,
my publisher's blurbs, my computer disks, there they
go, all the garbage into the trash, go into the other
offices, take advantage of lunch hour, ditch as much as
possible, four trashbags, this hallway isn't wide
enough, couldn't do much more than these five trashbags, I've always had a problem with hallways, when I

was four, Dad made me visit the new apartment where we were going to live, without Mom, Mom was gone, she'd left, he showed me my room full of new toys, his office right next door, and the only thing I was interested in, I remember, was the hallway, is there a hallway big enough to play with toy cars and to play shop? Measure the hallway, how many steps to the door, look at that, more coming back than going, begin again, go back and sit down, no, first take the bags downstairs, my head is spinning, it's making a huge noise, it's spinning and pounding, I want some cat-tube tea, cats again, I'm sick of cats, the tea is too hot, burns my tongue and throat, another gulp, just right for me, I just had to be friendly, friendly and unleavable, I was his little bear.

We were in the bathroom, I remember. I was his little bear. I was jealous of that girl, Paula, who was going out with his father and whom we'd watched arriving, the-world-belongs-to-me type and guys do too, one morning, at the Porquerolles house. He was taking a bath. He thought it was funny I was jealous. He said but darling, she's my stepmother, you can't be jealous of my stepmother! That made me laugh, but still I was jealous, I thought she flirted too much, she was with his father but I'd seen her, at the beach, at the café, at the dinner table, acting interested and innocent, simpering, picking up all the men in the vicinity, oh how fascinating you are, how seductive you are, I thought she was beautiful and dangerous with that immobile face, as if sculpted out of wax, when she smiled her bones sort of moved to reveal her teeth, all identical, all the same size, I thought she was beautiful and bionic, with the look of a killer.

When I was fifteen she was already a model, I was fascinated by that perfect face, later on I learned it was fake, she'd picked it out on a computer with her surgeon, voilà, we'll make you have high cheekbones, just like that, with silicone, we can shorten your nose and add a little more to the chin for the equilibrium of the profile, the eyes are fine, nothing to change with the eyes, but we can perform a very slight incision on the temples to heighten the eyebrow line, what do you think, a few Botox injections to freeze it all, for your teeth you can consult my colleague. I liked that, deep down, deciding on your face like that, I thought it was classy.

Adrien was washing his hair, he had made his hair into a funny shape with the shampoo, bangs in the air on one side, it made me laugh, he said you don't need to be jealous, you're a billion times more beautiful than she is, she's all remade, frozen, she's the Terminator that girl, you know what she said to me, at the airport, when I went with Dad to pick her up and I wanted to help her carry her suitcase, she said thanks, I don't need anyone, I castrate men right away, and anyway now that she's with my father she isn't a woman anymore, she's taboo, that's how it is. I was reassured, I must have been stupid, or crazy, to be jealous of a taboo, and he wouldn't love me if I was stupid and crazy. Do you love me, tell me, do you love me? He loves me, he tells me he loves me, he'll prove it he swears it, he says look, we're like two fingers on the same hand, we're like that, look. Damn. Stupid hallway, I blink my eyes I have a piece of dust in my eye, I should have been suspicious, I'm never suspicious.

This complicity between them, which slightly worried his father, stop that you two, he'd say, when he saw them acting too friendly, or putting sunscreen on each other's backs, or singing in chorus after dinner. That made me smile, it was a sickly smile but still a smile, not jealous not jealous, he wouldn't love me if I was crazy, I wasn't crazy, I wasn't jealous, I should have been. But even then, what would that have changed? Would I have left? Maybe I wouldn't even have left. That was the end, in any case. We weren't children anymore and we loved each other the way

children do, with kicks, punches, pillow fights, children
children, children, I hate children, I hate love, I blink
my eyes, I'm not crying, no, no, I just have some dust
in my eye, I'm in my office, before, when I was still
with Adrien, I would never have been in my office at
that hour, I was sleeping with my fists closed, that's
why I was his little bear, he couldn't even be bothered
to find out why I was sleeping all day, what an asshole.
I have a stupid fucking piece of dust in my eye. Is it
from thinking about that girl who acted like my friend,
and who called me Nice Ass, how's it going Nice Ass?
One day I met her at the pool, she had already been
with Adrien but I didn't know it, not jealous, not
crazy, not jealous of a taboo, she said to me with her
Terminator smile and her formalin face people are stupid, they're all jerks, they're saying I slept with your
husband, you're both so cute, you're such a pretty
couple, you'd have to be really low to destroy so much
happiness, happiness is such a rare thing.

Go into the bathroom, rinse my contact lens, watch
out, don't let it fall, a few years ago on the Rue de
Condé I rubbed my eyes and lost one like that, usually since they're semi-hard they make a little sound
when they fall on the floor, I waited without moving
for the sound but it didn't come, I looked in the mir-

ror to make sure it hadn't stayed on the white of the
eye, or was stuck somewhere on my eyelashes, I turned
my eye in every direction, it wasn't on the white or the
eyelid or anywhere, so I began to panic, I crawled from
the bathroom to the living room feeling the ground
carefully, maybe it had fallen off on the way, it hadn't,
I began to cry, and since that wasn't helping anything
I stopped right away. Adrien came at that instant, he
found me on the ground next to the sofa caressing the
floor and sniffling, What's happening, I lost a contact,
What? How? If I don't find it I can't go to your stupid
conference, What? Why not? Because I can't see anything, But don't you have a spare, No don't you realize if I had a spare I wouldn't be crawling around like
this, Oh that's clever and how come you still don't
have a spare contact, since you're so myopic? I don't
know you're getting on my nerves, But it's a catastrophe,
Shut up it's not a good time for this it's a catastrophe
but it's not a good time, You shouldn't have rubbed
your eyes angel, I know I shouldn't have but what
good is it telling me what I should or shouldn't have
done it's too late it's done. I was screaming, I was furious, he was annoying me so much I wasn't thinking
about my contact anymore, he looked at me startled
and suddenly he said don't move, he put his dusty

fingers over my eyelid, pulled it up and delicately removed the lens that was clinging to an eyelash. I rinse my contact. I put it back on my eye. In a few years the operation for extreme myopia will be perfected, but in a few years, bingo, I'll be far-sighted, how awful, plus I'll have wrinkles and everything, I look at myself in the mirror, I don't have wrinkles, I look sick.

six

The bathroom, jealousy, the shampooed bangs sticking
out, the clarifications, the kindness, the little bear, all
that was two years ago, or three, it was yesterday, and
now he has a child with her, the beautiful nasty imperi-
ous Paula. It's the most wonderful day in my life he told
me on the phone, taking care to pause afterwards to hear
what my reaction would be. The Ingush of the Caucasus
are happy too when they have a baby, Dad told me to
console me. That made me laugh, the Ingush. And I did-
n't really need to be consoled, actually, since it didn't
matter much to me, at the time, that he had a baby.
Every time he called me I said okay, what is it this time?
Did he go to bed with his professor? His psychiatrist?

His psychiatrist's wife? So whether he had a baby or not didn't matter much. I was a little surprised, just a little, I should have been flabbergasted but I wasn't really, I waited for some kind of emotion, standing next to the telephone, after I hung up, but nothing came, nothing, like in the end, with amphetamines, when I'd become too used to them, too intoxicated for them to have any effect on me. Adrien wasn't yet dead for me, at that phase. He died later, with Pablo. Back then, he was just at the idiot stage. But I was the one that must have been dead, or too wounded to suffer any more, or in such a state of shock that nothing could affect me anymore.

He used to say to me, when we loved each other, someday you'll leave me. That made me laugh, it was absurd, I replied no I won't leave you. Yes you will, you'll leave me because you're a queen and I'm nothing, you don't give a damn about anything, you don't care what people say about you or what they think, you don't care if people like you or not, you don't need me, you don't need anyone, you're strong, stronger than I am actually. I laughed, that made me scream with laughter, stronger than him, don't need anyone, what a joke. But he kept stubbornly repeating I'd leave him someday, I'm sure of it, but I'm also sure no one

will ever love you the way I do. Oh yes, why's that?
Because. Because why? Because that's how it is, I know
you by heart, I love you by heart, no one will ever love
you by heart the way I do. I thought he was wrong. It's
a long time ago, I don't remember very well, but I
think I thought he was wrong, that we'd never leave
each other, he was my whole life, I wasn't going to
leave my life, he said that to make himself afraid, and
it made me dizzy to imagine myself without him. He
said that to hurt himself, to hurt me, but it didn't hurt,
it was like trying to imagine a color that doesn't exist,
I couldn't manage it.

I didn't cry the day he left me. I was dying to, I was
full of tears inside, drowned in tears inside, inside I
was screaming, but in front of him I didn't cry. I
didn't cry in front of Mom either. She wasn't sick yet,
or she didn't know it yet, but she was so sad, almost
as sad as I was maybe, she loved him so much, not as
I did but she loved him so, she didn't understand it
either, so she came to my place, she stroked my hair
for a long time, she rolled me a joint and I fell asleep.
The next morning, I called him on his cell phone.
That's it then, you're gone, really gone? Yes, that's it,
I'm really gone. There was so much kindness in his
voice, so much incredulity too, it seemed so hard for

him to believe it himself, I sensed so much pleading in
his way of repeating I love you, I love you so much,
forgive me, forgive me, forgive me, that I still didn't
cry and I wasn't even angry at him. We stayed on the
phone for a long time without speaking, just breathing
with our hearts beating, still together, still in the same
rhythm, a little, oh please a tiny little bit, like two
Siamese twins just separated, like a headless body that
keeps running, like a bodyless head that keeps giving
its death rattle, still, a few instants, one last cuddle,
one last fix, one last sigh, the end. We were quiet, there
was too much to say, we understood each other so well
when we didn't say anything, we understood each
other best in silence, finally.

In the silence now, I don't hear anything. My head
is pounding, but I don't hear anything else. Stretch out,
stretch out one leg, let the other one join it, stop moving, see, we were like that, like two legs, two fingers,
two twins, two inseparables, it's my office, I have a
right, I even have the right to fall asleep if I want to, to
talk out loud by myself, to sing a stupid song, to clench
my teeth, to say and think nothing at all, maybe I
didn't have a right to do what I did with the manuscripts, but oh well, I feel better, I feel a tiny bit less
sick, it's pounding less inside my head, the dentist told

me I was wearing down my teeth because I was clenching my jaws together. Did I realize I was clenching my
jaws? Maybe, at night, so as not to talk, so as not to
say anything to Adrien who had taped me once, when
I was too talkative in the middle of a dream. I had
thought that was so violent of him, not like a rape but
like a theft, the theft of my voice, my dream and my
breathing on a tape, that, to take revenge, I read his
diary. No, actually, that's not true, I had read his diary
before that. He wrote that he loved me, saying things
like that don't mean anything. He wrote he loved me,
the rest I didn't read, or else I forgot it. I feel sick again.
I want a cigarette. I know, I smoke too much. I'll stop
when I'm pregnant. I took some time getting to this
point, but now it's done, I smoke too much. Smoking
is finished. Getting married is finished. Getting divorced
is finished. What's left? Driver's license, voting registra-
tion card, and, yes, having a baby.

The divorce went quickly, I had forgotten the date,
I always forget dates, I don't like dates, I hate the date
of my birthday, same with that date, the date of that
crummy divorce from that shitty guy I loved so much.
I think you should have the right to choose the date of
your birthday, it's such a small thing to ask, like Paula
and her face. I told Pablo I was a Scorpio, I thought

that was sexy, sexier than Virgo, I chose a great day in November, and then I forgot it, but he didn't, so he had a bunch of flowers delivered to my place, that's not what you say a bunch of flowers, what's the phrase? A bunch of bouquets, no, bunch isn't right, some bouquets, he had some bouquets delivered to my place sometime in November, I was happy, surprised but happy. I'd read my horoscope every week, in *Elle*, out loud. So, what's going to happen to us Scorpios? I internalized everything, I liked deciding my future, like when I was thirteen and I had a tattoo put in my hand to prolong my lifeline. Sometimes I'd read Virgo in passing, skimming over it not out loud, just to see what I was oops escaping.

Maybe I thought that by forgetting the divorce date I would escape it. But for that he'd have to forget it too. But he doesn't forget anything, he's hypermnesic. He always said he should have his memory bled every once in a while. Sometimes he sends me photos of us, I don't know where he gets them from, he must have put them in storage, we're in Rome with Ben and the kitten we forgot there, we're in Amsterdam in front of a poster "nobody makes them like my mum does," we're in Jamaica completely stoned with giant cigars on a giant pedal boat. He keeps everything. He forgets nothing. So the divorce... When he called me on his cell phone, somewhere I don't know when, I was buying myself a new pair of jeans, that I remember but it doesn't help me with the date, he was hopping mad. What the hell are you doing? He bawled. He was waiting for me in front of the court house, in a black suit, almost the same one he wore the morning of my grandmother's funeral, or maybe the same, his important-event suit, I think if I had met him there for the first time, furious but with his hair carefully done, English cigarettes, polished shoes, nothing out of place, I wouldn't have liked him. I was in jeans, out of breath, bewildered, he wouldn't have liked me either. We signed the papers in the judge's office, it was easy, nice and quick, we had joint ownership of nothing except ourselves.

I gave everything away from my previous life, now I only wear jeans, I'm an ex-wife, ex-woman. An ex-woman-in-a-dress goes against the grain, or it's a disguise and you have to be extremely well-grounded to wear a disguise, not to be afraid of losing yourself, to be well aware of where you are and what you are, I'm Adrien's ex-wife, the ex-granddaughter of my grandmother and I have telescopic legs, Pablo told me that, and he'd like me to wear a dress, sometimes, so I say we'll see, we have time, all the while knowing very well that dresses are for real women, otherwise it's a travesty, for transvestites, anyway it's not for me. Afterwards, we went to have a coffee opposite the courthouse, he was sniveling, he was getting on my nerves with his dark glasses he wore to let on he was sad, I didn't cry, for a long time now it had stopped making me cry, making me sad.

He was sad too, Pablo, when he read my real birthday date on my passport. We were overexcited, we were leaving for Morocco, he kept saying Africa! Africa! The African continent! I thought he was cute but I didn't say anything, he hates the idea that I find him cute, it offends him, I didn't want to offend him, but he was offended that I had lied to him, or maybe disappointed that I wasn't a Scorpio, he didn't say anything but from time to time, on the plane, he looked sideways at me like who is this girl, this is crazy. Over the desert, I tried to reassure him, you know I have Scorpio rising, that's good too, it's almost better, but I saw he didn't believe me anymore, that's too bad, for once I wasn't lying, I felt completely naked for not lying.

seven

Rue Bonaparte is where my apartment is, I looked for it for a year, after I broke up with Adrien. I looked and looked, everything looked good, I liked everything, I didn't have any criteria anything to compare them to, I asked my girlfriends, what do you think, what's your opinion, I pretended to be offhand and cheerful, I pretended it was fun looking for an apartment, with Adrien we didn't enjoy it, we had money problems, we were proud, we didn't want to ask our fathers for money for the security deposit, or rather he didn't want to, I couldn't care less, I don't have that kind of pride or shame, and of course our fathers were the ones who took care of the deposit in the end.

For the Rue Bonaparte place I didn't have money problems, but I was alone. Free, idiotically free, like Buridan's ass. Before, my freedom was Adrien. Now that Adrien had left, freedom was a void. I was all alone, my friends all had different opinions, and I didn't have any, so that didn't help me much, too big for what, too far from whom, too chichi, too hippie, too bourgeois, and what am I going to do in it anyway? Poor little rich girl, Mom said as a so-called joke, but I was mortified. That's a pretty strange reproach. I was her own daughter. Poor and rich, she's the one who made me that way. Poor and rich with her, with Dad, the campsite in Locmariaquer and the Parisian hotel rooms where Dad lived when he had a bunch of different women who all wanted me to call them Mommy, it made me dizzy in the end. For the apartment, I had the money, but I didn't have any ideas or any imagination, that's what annoyed me and worried my father, it's terrible to make your father worry, there's nothing more troubling than worrying a father who's already worried sick when he thinks about the misfortunes of his Louise, oh God things aren't going well with her, she isn't getting any better I can see it in her eyes. If only for that reason I prayed I'd find an apartment quickly I could pretend to like.

I get to a place, do I like it, can I see myself living there, with whom, painted what colors, what kind of music, with what desires, what habits, but it's as if I were stuck on a merry-go-round, which turned, and turned, and didn't stop, how to get off, how to stop it, how to regain my footing, everything was spinning around me, and my head spun with it, I wasn't unsure, I wasn't demanding or dreaming or rejecting. I was in a void, not a sleepwalker not a zombie, no, just empty, floating, a little out of it, like my grandmother on her answering machine. I knew I had to decide. There are a lot of things you like more than others, Dad had told me, what is it, what's wrong, nothing, Dad, every-thing's fine, look, look at this apartment on the Rue Bonaparte, it's a great apartment.

Ever since I was born and started to speak, it's always been the same record: What's wrong? Nothing, Dad, everything's fine, I'm your little Louise and every-thing's fine, even if inside there's nothing but empti-ness, or chaos, or Russian mountains, or a wish to cry out help help like the day I took a Darvon because I had a toothache, and because you were going to get married again but especially because I had a toothache, then another one because the pain was still there, and then another one, then all four packs finally, and I was already falling asleep and I kept repeating on the phone, like a stupid little robot, really, Dad, everything's fine, I swear everything's fine.

The only thing I was sure of is that I couldn't stay on Rue Bréa, with its dead, empty rooms, not a good kind of emptiness that's waiting to be filled, but a messy emptiness, a dirty emptiness, rooms I didn't vacuum anymore, where even my cats had stopped setting foot. The emptiness of Adrien's library, the emptiness of his hurried and carefully thought-out departure, early in the morning, with just a little suitcase, the emptiness of his flight, of his office, of his cupboards, an emptiness full of those details, when I came across them, a few days later, one night, as I hurried to close the shutters that were banging in the storm, they made me nauseous. An envelope, pieces of a photograph that slipped out of the trash, his face, my hand, a shape in a canary-yellow raincoat in the rain, I think it was in Venice, I think it was a raincoat they'd lent me at the hotel, I think this image of me hidden under the much too big sailor's raincoat moved me to tears, I had forgotten he'd taken this picture of me, then taken me in his arms murmuring it was the prettiest picture he'd ever have of me, and this is the photograph he forgot when he left since there it is, torn to shreds, in his office, her ex-husband's ex-office.

There was also a book cover, a shoelace, a dumbbell, a scarf, a snow boot, a hairbrush, in that room empty as a pillaged tomb, an emptiness that was like the one in my head, in my belly, an emptiness that would never be filled, that would have resisted the arrival of new furniture new objects new feelings, that emptiness absorbed everything like a black hole, it was an inter-galactic emptiness, a dense emptiness, a monstrous emptiness, I had to leave, I had to decontaminate myself right away, that's it, Rue Bonaparte, that's all I thought when I visited it and made up my mind, I didn't say to myself this is it, it's my style, my ideal, it's a pretty cocoon for a pretty new life, I hate people who tell themselves that, I can't stand people who spend their lives looking for the perfect place where they could settle down and, once they've found it, do a ton of things to fix it up right, when they're done it's over, they've become old, all they have left is to die, no, I just told myself it's a good apartment because it's a good decontamination airlock.

eight

I don't have any likes. No dislikes either, really. I know what's done and what's not done, I know the ins and outs, but that leaves room for leeway, massive room, and inside me too there's massive room and that's why it's empty, there's nothing there and I'm still waiting.

I'm waiting for my likes to come, or come back, like a lost appetite, or sleep for an insomniac. I had a lot of likes when I was little, I must have liked red more than green, yes, now I remember, I couldn't stand green, and the idea of orange and green together was enough to make me want to puke. But now I close my eyes, I imagine orange and green orange and green, still the desire to puke doesn't come, I've lost my disgust.

So I wait. I observe. I open my eyes wide every time I visit someone's place, is it beautiful, do I like it, wow how nice it is here! I force myself, that might help things, you'd think I liked it, but it doesn't really help much, it's been a year now that I've been on the Rue Bonaparte and I still haven't found what I liked.

Before it was simple. I liked what Adrien liked. He liked black and white, he thought colors were horrible and vulgar and I acted like him, exactly like him, it was so simple. Once, to act like him, I painted all my books black, it didn't help recognizing them later on, but life isn't made to be helpful, and I loved Adrien.

When I moved, I asked Mom to help me. She had taste, she has taste, maybe it's even my taste after all, who knows, that would settle everything, but maybe not, how can you tell? I told myself we'll see, like all the rest, like love, like dresses, like the parties I went to crying but in the end I was happy, and so I called Mom. You have to take the walls down, she said, remove the doors, all the doors, even the bathroom door? Even the bathroom door, and then the urgent thing, the absolutely urgent thing, is the moldings on the ceiling, they're so bourgeois, down with moldings, and then the real problem in apartments is or-ga-ni-za-tion-of-the-space. I agreed, I agreed with everything,

I sensed it was a taste and it was enough to say it was my taste, taste in a kit, pre-fabricated taste, occupant-ready, anything is better than the nothingness I was shut up in, which for the first time was beginning to make me panic a little.

Mom introduced me to a friend of hers, an architect decorator. True, he was at least a hundred years old, he'd just gotten out of prison, he came from Albania, he didn't have any legal residency papers, but in his country he was the king, the leader in non-bourgeois interior decorating. He began by breaking down a door with a hammer, he seemed very happy, very much in agreement with Mom, he seemed to be taking immense pleasure in smashing up my door. Then, since another door resisted, he used his feet and his fists, I said but Mr. Roussovitch, he kept banging away, bang bang, but Mr. Roussovitch maybe we don't have to break down all the doors, bang bang, I could put them in the basement in case I changed my mind, he stopped banging, he glanced at me suspiciously, he crushed out his cigarette butt on the floor, and he said something to me in Albanian. I said Sorry, come again, he repeated the same thing with big gestures as if he were jumping rope, and then pointed his finger at me again, threateningly. I said Okay okay, he nodded his head and went on demolishing everything. The next day he didn't come back, he didn't ask to be paid, not a cent, we never saw him again.

Is the most urgent thing the moldings? I asked Mom. I think the urgent thing is not to take things away but to add things, sheets, curtains, frills fans screens. But she didn't agree, moldings first, and she got angry, and she told me in that case you're on your own. I said oh well, I'll manage and I managed.

I wanted to buy some curtains, or maybe blinds, which do I prefer? I didn't prefer anything, so I just tacked some sheets up over the windows to protect the neighbors, so they didn't see me naked all the time. I went to the Salvation Army and unearthed a big rustic wooden table, it was the only one there and I needed a table, and also it looked like the table at my grand-mother's place, I had my seat reserved next to hers, on a booster seat, I wouldn't let anyone else sit there, it was my spot, it was a good ritual, a good habit. I also took a mattress that looked like it had never been used. And then at Darty I let the appliance guy trick me into buying an immense fridge for an immense family, after all, maybe someday that'll happen to me, an immense family and lots of habits. And then finally at Ikea, I came across a super-cute salesman who intimidated me, which made me lose my cool even more: I began explaining to him that I was color-blind, he had to choose for me, and then I changed my mind, I picked out a hammock, an inflatable globe, and a rocking chair, very quickly, without hesitating, as if I knew exactly what I wanted.

It's a real capharnum at your place, my father said, a week later, when he came to visit for the first time. I was mortified and I went to look it up in the dictionary, to see what he had meant. A jumble of odds and ends, the dictionary said. Okay. I like that expression, odds and ends, "bric and brac," it's like the names of two friends, or two twins, Bric and Brac, Adam and Eve and Pinch Me, and I forgave Dad. I let him give me an old sofa that reminded me of the time when I lived at his place. It was the sofa I had stretched out on when he bawled me out because I'd gotten bad grades in Latin, or because I skipped school. He was sitting on the sofa, pen in hand, when he asked me what about your midterm report card, why haven't I gotten your midterm report card? He had gotten it, actually, but I had intercepted it, I had tried to doctor the grades, but it showed too much, so I said to him, that day, that there was no midterm. What? What kind of drivel is that? It's not drivel, it's true, this year you see, they got rid of midterm, it was the guidance counselor's decision, it's an experiment. What's your guidance counselor's name? Uh, I dunno, I never had any actual dealings with him. Well find out, I'd like to hear that gentleman explain that to me, make an appointment for me. Yes, Dad. I left his office, tears in my eyes, the report-card story was so as not to disappoint him, my grades were really mediocre, 0.5 average in Latin, 3 in history, 2 in math, and then the teachers' comments, too scattered, that is if she even takes the trouble of coming to class, her refusal to learn prevents her intelligence from developing, that would have devastated him, I didn't want him to be devastated, I left his office, the felt-tip pen he'd let fall on the sofa stained it with a little pool of green ink that's still there, today, it reminds me of my adolescence, it wasn't so bad, adolescence.

And then there was the business of the bed. What's happened to your bed, he asked me, the day they gave us the keys, didn't you have a bed before? I gave it away. Gave it away? Why? To whom? To the cleaning lady, because it was our marriage bed, and everything else too, everything was from our marriage so I gave it all away, didn't you do things like that too when you were my age, the apartment on the Rue Monge for instance, the one I was born in, that you sold in ten minutes to the company on the ground floor, to have some money to go skiing with Mom. No, that's not true, I didn't dare say that to him, I just thought it, but what nerve he's got to bawl me out like that, for a bed. No, that's not really true either, he didn't really bawl me out, I'm no longer the right age to be bawled out, he probably thinks there's no use in it anymore, he can't change me anymore, it's too late, all my habits have been formed, my bad habits. That made me a little sad, the first time I realized that, because before, he'd bawl me out then console me, and it was good, being consoled, it was childhood, children don't choose, you choose for them, children aren't left, aren't deceived, aren't abandoned, just scolded.

Or rather they are, Mom left me when I was four years old, she brought me to the Twickenham, where Dad had his trysts, with my big brown suitcase, my mini leather jacket and the plastic bag they give children on airplanes that I never let go of, even when I went to sleep, but, one slight difference, but a huge slight difference, she didn't leave me for someone else, for some other child she preferred over me, she left me for good, for my own happiness, and because someday she'd come back. Adrien left me for someone else. Adrien won't come back. That's what it is to be an adult. Being an adult means being replaceable.

nine

I met Pablo on a boat. It's a trap, I said to myself, when a boy I liked who wasn't yet Pablo came looking for me saying there's a party on a boat, come on, I have a Zodiac, I'll take you. As the Zodiac drew close, I said to myself what am I going to do to get away, how can you get away when you're cooped up in the middle of the sea, and I was petrified. I would so like to have seemed arrogant, sure of myself! I would so like to have resembled those happy, handsome ex-children I used to envy when I was little because they didn't have any worries and they had lots of friends, on their birthday their mothers organized parties where the whole class was invited, even the teacher sometimes, and all the cousins, and there were toys, cakes, balloons, framed photos of their parents on their wedding day, in the living room everything's in its place, the sofa, the coffee table, the knickknacks, the paintings. My childhood wasn't like that. I had the tenderness and love children need to grow up. But I don't have any cousins, and I can't act arrogant.

The people on the boat were nice. Introductions were made, we all greeted each other, I had taken out my contacts from shyness and there were only tanned shapes, striped with white, the white of their teeth, of their smiles and of the sky, a blinding white. It was lunchtime. Everyone was sitting around a table. That bothered me too much, getting settled in like that, with them, so close, caught between the water and the sky, trapped between them, water and sky, to have to eat, talk, to say what, to reply how, to blush, to try to lessen the blush by pinching the lobe of my ear, not to know what to do with my hands, my legs, my hair, with me, all tangled up in knots. I said I'm not hungry thanks, and I stayed all alone on the cushion in the stern, smoking cigarettes.

I had brought a book with me, *I Am a Cat*, because of the title but it was unreadable and I thought I was being ridiculous being so afraid and reading that.

Afraid of what, you wonder. I liked him, that's true, the boy who wasn't yet Pablo who had come looking for me in his Zodiac, but not that much, not to the point of being so afraid. I could hear them laughing, over there. They must have thought her pretty weird, that guest who, under the pretext she wasn't hungry, doesn't even want to sit down at table. I wanted to take off my jeans, but I had forgotten my bathing suit, that was stupid, it made me laugh all by myself, so that we were laughing at the same time, them out loud, me quietly, that's good, it was a beginning, it was almost laughing together and it reassured me.

After lunch the guests came astern and each found their place again. That has always stunned me this way people have of always finding their place wherever they are, right away, as if their spot were waiting only for them and it was the most obvious thing in the world. I never know where my place is. Then, by chance, I had succeeded in not taking anyone else's place on the big cushion that covered the rear deck and they sat down around me. Someone put a on a CD, a song that said I aaaam a baby elephant that's gone astraaaay. A long leggy girl lent me a blue bathing suit, I almost told her I'd lost my suitcase in the airport and that's why etcetera, but she didn't seem to expect any explanations, it was windy, sunny and watery, there was a boy I liked, I was finally almost happy, to everyone around me and to the void I smiled, little smiles that meant I'm someone nice, I'm not so afraid anymore, don't worry about me, I'm not going to steal anyone's fiancé, voices took a while to reach me, maybe because of the wind, or my myopia, I always hear less well when I can't see anything, I was listening but what I heard didn't mean anything, and also the voices melted into each other, I had swallowed a few tablets of Xanax on the side and the voices became a murmuring, then a nursery rhyme, the sweet happy nursery rhyme my grandmother used to sing to me in the morning when I brushed my teeth, long live water, long live water, that washes us and makes us clean, long live water, long live water, that washes us and makes us fair, I smiled blissfully and blissfully I fell asleep, an arm folded over my face, I didn't want to run away anymore.

When I woke up, everyone was sleeping around me, carefree as babies. It was a siesta, this party. Or a big nursery. I went below looking for shade and aspirin, and to put on my contacts, finally. In the cabin the boy I liked was sleeping, but I just liked him a little bit, calmly, because I knew I would never love him and there was this void in me that prevented me from ever loving anyone as I had loved Adrien. I liked him the way you like a fruit or a song, the way I think he liked me too. Or rather, no, he wasn't sleeping. With his eyes open, fixed on me, he got up, said something to me that I didn't understand, what? He repeated it, I still didn't understand, but I didn't dare insist and I went into the little bathroom. All of a sudden, I felt his arms around me. He turned my head towards him and kissed me, like that, as if it was the only thing to do, as if it went without saying. Then I turned around completely and put my hands on his temples, where the blood beats strongest, and I kissed him too. He was salty, I had never kissed anyone so salty, I remembered Adrien's skin, in Brindisi, it was so hot we never left the hotel before nightfall, we stayed stretched out under the fan, face to face, blinds closed, he said to me come, come, opening his arms, I was happy, his skin was salty too, it wasn't sea salt, it was the salt of sweat on his skin still a child's, we weren't even twenty yet, we loved each other but we didn't know what that meant, we didn't know that meant we were going to suffer, we were going to cry and fight and hurt each other and want to die, we had seen other people like that but we weren't other people, we were a miracle, we were going to win out where Ariane and Solal had failed, we were living in the instant, we didn't ask ourselves questions, we didn't know that one day love would become a memory that wrenches your heart.

I blotted out Adrien and kissed him again, the salty boy, his beard, his mouth, his nose, his hair, his whole face, I was happy, voracious and happy, and then the girl who had lent me her swimsuit came into the cabin and she didn't look at all happy, not at all. She looked at us without saying anything, first at him, then at me, then at him, she was beautiful, something old-fashioned about her face, and vague, but that must have been my contacts, and she went out. Her look at him didn't reveal anything. Except, maybe, a slight fatigue. I said what's wrong with her? He looked surprised and, without replying, brought his face close to mine. I said no, I'm not kissing you anymore. You won't kiss me anymore? No. I went out. I found the girl. She was sitting on a cushion, her long legs folded up under her arms, as if she had wanted to turn tail and run and had decided not to, you could see she had just been crying, she stared at my breasts, no, stupid, she stared at her swimsuit on my breasts and I felt like a slut. I wanted to say something to her I didn't know what, don't worry, it was just a kiss a kiss is nothing at all but I didn't have the strength to lie to her: How many boys had I kissed in my life? Five, yes five, or rather six now, so it wasn't true, it wasn't true that a kiss was nothing at all, so I didn't say anything, I felt fatigue swooping down on me again, I felt sick and I didn't have the courage to do anything. Do you have a cigarette? She asked me. I said they're up above, come on. So we both climbed back up onto the deck.

The siesta was over. Everyone was dancing to a strange song, I thought it was undanceable, a song that talked about Brussels and made me reel, or maybe it was just the boat, in any case everyone was dancing, out of time with each other, without touching each other or talking, but you could see they were all together, like a family, like friends, like everything I didn't have anymore and that I missed when I thought about it but fortunately I didn't always think about it, in fact I think it's been two years now I've thought only about not thinking about it, they weren't dancing very well, and not very rhythmically, but they danced in the same off-beat tempo and I looked at them, or rather I looked at their legs so as not to meet their eyes, so that one of them wouldn't meet my eyes and say come on, why don't you come dance, I'd have replied no thanks, I'm tired, like before no thanks I'm not hungry.

I wasn't smiling anymore. I was wondering when I'd go home. I told myself that in my room at my hotel, I'd dance all by myself, just for me, and that desire would return to me just like that. I told myself that I'd put on a different kind of music, a music I liked, what do I like, what do I love, my records were Adrien's and I broke them all in half, all of them, it was hard, they were solid, but I broke them, methodically, calmly, Prince, the Stones, Cat Stevens, the Red Hot Chili Peppers, the records we smoked grass to, the soundtrack from *Rocky* he put on in the morning to lift weights, I liked Rocky but I liked Jeanne Moreau better, can you dance to Jeanne Moreau? Anyway that doesn't change anything, Adrien said I couldn't walk in front of a mirror without blushing up to my ears, so all alone or not all alone, what does that change in the end?

The shadows were getting longer, everyone was dancing, and I twisted every which way to put my jeans back on without getting up. As I was twisting around I remembered how good it was when my grandmother forced me to go out, go on, go dancing, have fun, and I swallowed down my tears, and gathered up all my remaining courage, and went out and I was happy, of course, in the end. A guy who was all stomach, with a poncho-like vest, came and sat down next to me, he

gave me a look that was so malignant and so black I
thought I was going to break out in tears, there, in
front of everyone, in front of the setting sun, on this
boat trapped in the middle of nowhere, and he said
why don't you ever look people in the eye? My eyes
began to sting me. A not very sexy tear began to drop
from the tip of my nose, which I wiped away with the
palm of my hand. What does this guy have against me,
with his piercing gaze? I blushed, coughed, sweated,
go away I thought, fuck off, but he didn't go away, he
held out a Kleenex with a menacing look. It's my contacts I said to him trying to look him right in the eye
but that made me tear up even more. What's that? My
contacts, it's because of my contacts. He'll understand
I told myself, with such a piercing look he'll have to
understand that it's because of my contacts that I don't
look people in the eye but just in the direction of their
eyes and that if I want to cry, it's because of the salt,
the sand, the sun and my whole life too. He took me
in his arms, then. He was my father's age and I let
myself go and be rocked, I cuddled up to him, I wanted
someone to be kind, just kind, you shouldn't be afraid
he said to me, no one wants to harm you, you should
look people in the eye, eye contact, you understand,
eye contact. He began to stroke my arm, I let him, he

impressed me, then my neck, then my stomach, stop I said, then my back, stop, then my breasts, damn, damn, eye contact, and then I pushed him away with all my strength, and he went crashing against the railing with a soft thud. That's when Pablo arrived, what's happening, what's happening, and he began to talk to me.

He was talking to me, but I wasn't listening to him, I was still thinking about the guy in the poncho, and then I looked at his hard mouth, the corners turned down, his big widely spaced eyes, clear transparent blue, without really seeing them, here's someone who understands intelligent, unusual things, I told myself, but he didn't intimidate me much, that was strange. What did that guy want with you? Nothing, I don't know, nothing, I stammered looking at his eyebrows so as not to see his eyes anymore and not risk blushing. He talked and talked, I wondered if he was going to kiss me too, but since he was talking I was relaxed, as long as he talked I didn't have anything to worry about, the sun was in his face and he scarcely blinked, I don't know what he was talking to me about, he was very vehement. I told myself I'm going to go back to Paris, I'm going to leave my boyfriend of the moment: Maybe deep down we're fine on our own, what do I know about it, I've never been alone, since Adrien I never slept alone, always someone there in the dead man's seat in my bed, since Adrien left, there have been five kisses and three lovers, I think. I let them choose me, approach me and try to please me, and I sometimes let them think they did please me, for the time it took for the next one to replace the one before. I expected nothing, I hoped for nothing, I decided nothing, I was neither happy nor sad, it was like the apartments: Why that one instead of some other one, I told myself we'll see. But maybe you're better off on your own? Yes, you can sleep crosswise on the bed, eat melba toast all night, listen to the same song in a loop a hundred times over, but then no more caresses, no more cuddles, no, you're definitely not better on your own, stretch out your arm in the big bed and find no one, not even someone who annoys me, not even someone who disgusts me, no one, no, that's definitely not better, I need someone to look after me, someone to love me or make me sick of him or get on my nerves or make me laugh, but also someone to leave me alone, what do I need more, for someone to look after me or leave me alone?

I interrupted him. He was in the process of mimicking something, or imitating someone. He had gotten up and was making big windmill motions with his arms. What's your name? He stopped, sat down next to me on the railing. Pablo. And you? Louise. He smiled, I loved his smile, very pointy canine teeth and his front teeth long and chalky-white, I liked them a lot, his teeth, I wanted to tell him that but he might have thought that strange, I was right not to say anything, since six months later when I told him that what I liked about him were his teeth, he almost left me. So I just said I think I like you. He swallowed his saliva, he looked right and left and, since he was bringing his head towards me, I said no no I don't want to kiss you. But, you just... Yes, but I don't want to kiss you. Oh okay. He looked right and left again, and at the sun that still didn't make him blink. The sun always made Adrien sneeze. With him, nothing, he just shrugged his shoulders. And then the boat stopped, everyone stretched, collective yawn, commotion with everyone looking for their shoes, did anyone see my *pareo*, where's my bra: It's true that we stayed sitting on the railing, our legs dangling, looking at each other; it's true he pleased me, not his teeth, but something in back of his eyes, a capacity for enthusiasm and astonishment I could guess at, a drive, an energy, something whole and childlike, not really childlike I hate men-children, something dense, clean, direct, alive. Around us, people were still bustling about, Pablo had stopped smiling. A guy with a toothbrush moustache came over to tap him on the shoulder and say meow meow laughing in his ear, I had thrown my book overboard but maybe he'd seen it, Pablo glared at him, the guy walked away, still laughing, and I blushed violently.

You have a sunburn, he said to me,

yes,

tonight we'll stay together,

I don't know,

we'll have dinner and go dancing at the Indio Malo and then there's a party and afterwards,

afterwards you'll come home with me,

no afterwards you'll sleep at home it's a big house, there are lots of rooms,

no, afterwards you'll come home with me.

but the party will last a long time, maybe all night, and I won't be able to drive, to bring you home on a scooter to the other end of the island, drunk as a pig.

as a pig?

as a pig.

are pigs forced to get drunk?

okay, listen, I don't want to bring you home, I want you to stay with me.

Come on, come on someone shouted, first batch for the Zodiac!

We got into the Zodiac, shoes in hand, the leggy girl and the salty boy I no longer liked holding each other by the hand again, and Pablo who I was beginning to like more and more, and some others, we were crammed in, piled on top of each other, another girl with a narrow face, eyes drawn up towards her temples and the rakish look of a wizened child sat down on my lap, someone with a beach towel on his head was imitating Mitterrand eating ortolans, someone else got completely naked and almost made us capsize and, as we were beaching the boat, we got attacked by a cloud of mosquitoes that must surely have been waiting for us. I was no longer floating. I was in the same net as everyone else, smiling like them, beneath the cloud of mosquitoes like them. Pablo took my arm to find shelter more quickly. I noticed that with him I ran more quickly. Afterwards, when we kissed each other, for the first time I didn't think of Adrien, I didn't think of anyone, I thought I was happy. And then very quickly we laughed, when we found ourselves in the big house, tangled up in the mosquito net, and it fell down, and before tearing it apart to free ourselves from it we kissed each other again and got even more tangled up.

ten

I returned to Paris, alone, two days before him. I didn't miss him. I didn't think about him. Pablo had never existed, not his chalk-white teeth, or his laugh, or his eyes that could look right at the sun without blinking, or the mosquito net, all that didn't exist, Pablo himself didn't exist, I didn't think about him. I didn't think about much, actually. I was in that strange state I know so well, which I still have again from time to time. Louise are you listening to me? Yes, I'm listening. But actually, no, I'm not listening, neither to the noise outside nor to the noise inside, I smoke cigarettes, I swallow Xanax pills like candies, it's magic, it creates a barrier, there's nothing but quiet, like cotton-wool, and this weight in my stomach, this ever-so-slight weight that makes me want to stay still without doing anything, not move. I didn't miss Pablo. His teeth, his laugh, his eyes, no no, it's as if I'd already forgotten them. So how was Formentera, Louise? Not bad, it wasn't bad. Was the weather nice? Yes very nice, I just had one CD, by Barbara, that was good, I love Barbara, I don't miss him.

And at the same time I wasn't so surprised either the day he phoned me. I was going out with one of those boys I didn't choose, I didn't dislike him but I didn't like him either, or rather it depended, in any case I wasn't treating him very well, his name was Gabriel. When he was nice, and he often was, I said to him I like you but I don't love you, don't even bother to have any hopes, there's nothing to be had from me, even if I get better someday you're not the one I'll love. He answered, with tears in the corners of his eyes, little tears that I envied and that filled me with disgust, he answered that's okay, I love you, it's important to be loved, it's a gift I'm giving you, I don't want anything in exchange. I didn't argue, maybe he was right, but I didn't give a shit. Sometimes I thought about leaving him, but for what reason? For somebody else with whom it would be just the same? I could have wound up with some asshole or nutcase instead of him, that was Mom's great terror when I was a teenager, I didn't wind up with anybody, I didn't have any breasts, I wore glasses and bangs, and Mom imagined me picking up an asshole or a nutcase, maybe that's what she hoped for deep down, maybe she said to herself my poor little Louise, isn't an asshole better than nothing?

One night, just before Pablo, I really wound up with an asshole. He was a fat but agile boy who followed me from the supermarket, about five blocks or so. I was leaving the psychoanalyst's, it was my second and final meeting, he had said something annoying to me (I was very annoyed) it's because your mother slept with your father, and I had thought that so violent that I ran out the door, then there's this guy following me! I stop in the middle of the street, what do you want I say? What is it? And the guy starts simpering, like a plump, shy girl, um, I just wanted to ask you out for some coffee or something.... Mollified but still irritated, but vaguely flattered all the same, that always reassures me, dope that I am, being followed in the street and hit on, I tell myself things have changed, I've changed, I'm no longer that puny, drab little girl men look at without seeing, I reply no thanks it's very nice of you but I don't like coffee. Then the guy changes completely.

Suddenly he's not the least bit shy. What makes you think I'm nice, bitch? I'm not nice! I cross the street, he crosses too. I speed up, he comes even with me. What a vulgar smile, I tell myself. That's the only thing I'll find to say to the cops, afterwards, when I press charges. I won't remember how he was dressed or the color of his hair or his eyes, I'll just say to them: He had a vulgar smile, he had a gap in his teeth. Come on, just a little drink, he muttered a little more softly but as obscenely as if he had said come on, just a little blow job, tapping me on the ass as he said it. I look at him. I slap him. And then he pounces on me and punches me right in the face.

I don't feel anything at first. I don't really understand what's just happened to me. I'm just on the ground, I have blood in my mouth and eyes, I think about my contacts, oh shit my contacts, without my contacts I'll never be able to get up and run away, and I feel a massive shape swooping down on me. It's the Arab man from the neighborhood who brought me back home. And, with the mirror two inches away to examine the damage, I make four silly phone calls. The optician, to order new contacts on the double. Adrien, that must have been a reflex, but I got his answering machine and a huge desire to cry overcame me as I hung up, a wish to cry harder than I've done in a long time. Gabriel (I've been attaaaaaacked!). And then Dad, obviously, who got nice and worried about me, as he should, and who calmed his big little crybaby down before going on to launch his red-alert to find the scumbag, have the neighborhood patrolled, and stick me with some bodyguard bruisers I ended up begging to leave me alone, please, gentlemen, stop following me everywhere like the other guy, go away, go away, we'll settle everything, I won't say anything to my father, and anyway he's not even here, he's on the other side of the world, he must have forgotten he hired you.

So, Pablo arrives and, with Pablo, I tell myself maybe things won't be entirely the same as before. Of course I don't love him. I tell myself I'll never love him, whatever he does, whatever he says, because love is atrocious, because love always stops one day and I never want to experience the death of love again. I'm not solid enough, I tell myself, not brave enough, not suicidal enough. I detest love, I repeat to myself, Adrien cured me of love for good. Love is always ugly, grotesque, pitiful, yuck, how can they all go around saying Albert Cohen's *Belle du Seigneur* is a great novel of love when it's just the opposite, and it shows how horrible love is? Anyway Pablo arrives. He lands in the middle of my edgy mean existence, and it's true I like him. I like him more than a pair of jeans, more than a song, more than I care to admit, I like him despite the double-bolts and suddenly there's a risk of love. Do I want to take this risk? Is it worth leaving behind me this choiceless life, where I don't have to decide anything, like a child, except a child has desires, whims, sorrows, and I don't feel anything, I let myself be carried along, rocked, caressed, Gabriel makes sure I eat, sleep, have some fun, it's comfortable, it's stupid, it's an almost fetal life, I have tiny little pleasures and minuscule upsets, I weep over a broken pen and take pleasure from a crust of bread dipped in tea, before that would have made me scream, before I would have had nothing but scorn for this kind of existence, Dad taught me to fight, since I was twelve years old, Dad always told me never put love first, never depend on a man, never depend on anyone, otherwise you'll be sorry, like X, like Y, like Z.

"You think I'm like X? or Y? or Z?"

"No, sweetheart, of course not, but you have to watch out, you have to toughen yourself."

"How do you do that, Dad, how do you go about toughening yourself?"

"You have to be less kind; it's good to be kind but you're so fragile, you have to be a little less kind. And read. Three books a week."

"But Dad, I'm already doing that!"

"I know, I know, that's good. But you have to do well on your *baccalauréat* exams, and to do that you have to read even more, write your notes down on cards before you go to sleep, don't dream about boys too much."

"Okay, Dad. But I have time for the exams, they're still five years away...."

"But those five years start from now. Afterwards it'll be too late."

"Okay."

"You say okay but you're thinking oh stop bothering me!"

"No, no I'm not thinking that, you never bother me, you know that."

Is there still time to toughen myself? Could I ever get by without a crutch, without Xanax, with my eyes wide open, facing life head-on? Even if I'm myopic? Even if, without my contacts, it's all a fog? Even if, when I hide behind my myopia, I have the impression that people see me as I see them, fuzzy, without outlines, and that, deep down, that suits me fine? It's hard with the world in your face. It's hard to see well, to listen well, to feel everything, without any filters. Could I live without my contacts? Are they not really protecting me after all? Will I ever experience time again the way it was before, when I wasn't afraid, when nothing was that serious, when no one died, when cancer happened only to writers, when Adrien was the man of my life, when Dad always settled everything?

I ask myself all that the day Pablo calls me up. Hello, he says, hello? And, very quickly, my heart beating, I see the mosquito net again, I hear again our nighttime laughter, I see again the blessed time on the boat, and I'm afraid, so afraid, and I tell myself that I won't know what to say to him. Hello? I reply. Hello? I can't hear you. And I hang up right away and go get Gabriel who's stretched out naked on my bed reading *Survival in Auschwitz* to admire my tan. Look, I have swimsuit marks, see, even the sun doesn't have a right to see my breasts, my ass. Who was that, he asks. My father, it was my father. He still doesn't know about us? He knows you exist, of course, but I told him you were a homo. And he believed you? Of course, he always believes me. So is everything okay? Yes, everything's fine. Louise? Yes? I bought you some good bread, the kind you like, look. That's nice but that's not the kind I like, it's revolting, it's sweet. I'm sorry, baby, please forgive me. Listen, I've already told you a thousand times I'm not your baby. You're not being very nice.

Yes I am, I am nice, stroke my back, no, my back, I said back, okay, stop you're tickling me, read me something instead, I don't have my contacts on. An hour goes by like that, someone rings the doorbell, and I go open it with just a big towel knotted over my breasts: It's Pablo.

"Um, Gabriel's here," I say smiling fixedly, outraged he came just like that, astonished he found my address, a little flattered too and, deep down, not completely surprised either.

Okay then what should we do? He asks, trying to open the door a little more with his foot.

I... I dunno!

Well I do.

Oh?

It's him or me.

Okay.

Him or me?

I don't know.

When will you know?

Tomorrow.

Why tomorrow?

Because.

What's going to happen between now and tomorrow?

Nothing...

So what then?

Okay then.

What okay?

Okay it's you.

It's me?

It's you.

Who's there? Gabriel shouts from the bedroom and Pablo pulls me towards him, kisses me on the neck, then whispers, taking my hand that's supposed to be holding up the towel and suddenly lets it drop, that he'll wait for me in a café nearby, but not all night.

I go back to the bedroom, my cheeks surely all red and scratched too by Pablo's beard. Gabriel looks at me, half-furious half-suspicious. Are you going to tell me again it was your father? I snatch the bubble pack of Xanax on my bedtable, swallow one pill, then another, okay, I say to him giving him my meanest look, I met someone. What? Who? Where? I met someone, I'm telling you, someone other than you, don't you understand what that means! And then he, with his Primo Levi still in his hand, his long eyelashes I liked to nibble when I was in a good mood blinking frantically, looks at me with a beseeching incredulity that disgusts me. I'm sick of his cowboy looks, his emotionalism, his kindness. That's exactly what I don't want to see anymore, this sensitive, desperate side. Is it someone I know? He asks dully, still stretched out, still naked. Oh no, this is going to take forever, I tell myself, I don't want that either, I don't want to explain myself, I don't want to go through the whole intense tearful thing, I just want it to be over, done with, finished, I just want him to clear off, scram, and never to hear about him again. No, I shout going into the bathroom, of course not, you don't know him, why do you always want to know everyone? I start the shower, the Xanax is beginning to take effect, I want to laugh, stupid laughter like when you smoke grass. What, you're still here? I say when I come back into the bedroom, also completely naked, suddenly without any shame, as if he'd stopped existing already. I throw his pants in his face, you can't stay! You have to leave! And then he leaps up from the bed and pins me to the wall by the throat.

"You can't do that, you can't make me leave just like that."

"Let me go, you're hurting me!"

"You're the one who's hurting me!"

"No, it's you, you're squeezing too hard, I'm suffocating."

Is he really going to strangle me? Is he capable of doing that? I remember him murmuring to me at night—

I pretended I didn't hear him—I want to build a wall around you. I remember his jealousy, and how he wanted to control everything in my life, my meals, my friends, my medication, my cats. When I wanted to annoy him, I'd run up the steps four at a time to put my key in the door before him, he couldn't bear it that I didn't need him even for that, he saw it as a defeat. I also think, very quickly, of how I'm hurting him, of this meanness that's just come over me, couldn't I have done that a little better, treated him better, pretended to suffer a little, or at least be attentive to his own suffering, not dismiss him like a dog, even with a dog I would have been kinder, but not now, with this absolute ingratitude, this monstrous egoism, is it so hard to lie a little, what would that have cost me, but no, dismissed, thrown out, mean spoiled little girl, mean violence that's so unlike me but that comes to me from so long ago, when I was a little girl who wasn't yet spoiled but who understood I had to choose Dad or Mom, or rather choose isn't the word, I loved Mom, but I knew that choosing Dad was choosing a normal life.

Yes, he's capable of it. He's definitely capable of strangling me. I stop struggling. He's too strong. Too angry. And then it's strange—the idea comes to me, then settles in my head, that it wouldn't really be such a bad idea. It would settle everything, no more decisions to make, no more choices, it would be over, everything would be over. After half a minute, though, he lets go, puts on his pants and leaves, slamming the door. It's over. I go find Pablo in the café where he was waiting for me. A little guilty of course, but not much, like an escapee, as if I'd broken a rule, but not a very serious rule, a little meaningless rule. Happy too to have chosen, to have had the strength to decide, that wasn't so hard really, that didn't hurt so much, it didn't even hurt at all. Did I think of the pain I caused Gabriel? No. I thought only of me, of the pain it wasn't causing me, exactly like it was when I left Mom. Savagery of hyper-sensitive children. Still I'll have to be careful, I just said to myself, I'll end up revealing what a monster I am.

eleven

I should be honest: I've taken some kind of medication all my life. Now I just drink tea but all my life I've taken something, maybe since Mom left, I'm not sure, or since I left Mom's place, I don't know how I should say it.

In the beginning, I'd say I have a headache and my grandmother would fix a glass of milk with some powder dissolved in it, she said you'll see, it's a placebo, it's magic, and it was magic, there was no better medicine in the world than this placebo.

Later on, when Mom told me I was born premature, after seven months, without eyebrows, without nails, without hair or eyelashes, and that she didn't let them put me in an incubator, I thought maybe I was missing something and I began to read all the medicine ads I could find, I was a rough draft of a little girl, a sketch of a girl, medications would complete me.

I also remember my Actifed period, when I kept taking cold tablets. I took one box a day. I explained I have a permanent runny nose, it's because of my cats, I'm allergic to my cats. You should have yourself desensitized the pharmacist told me, or try homeopathy. Yes, yes, I'll try it, I replied, but I'd still like four boxes of Actifed. I knew it wasn't normal to take medication for an illness you don't have. But I said to myself it's good, I'm being kind to myself, I'm taking care of myself, I just need a placebo, a ritual, a habit, like when I was with my grandmother, what harm can placebos do? I must even have dreamed, the day of Adrien's socialite tears, and of Dad's terrible tears, and of the continuous streams of Mom's tears, and of all the other tears, those of my friends, my little brother I could no longer console, I think I must have dreamed, that day, about a medication that can make you cry on the day of your grandmother's funeral....

I have to be honest, then. I can't put all the blame, all the responsibility, on other people. I have to admit, if I think about my drug-addicted period, that I had some previous history of it.

Still. It was after the abortion that I *really* began to believe I was missing something: I wasn't woman enough, not adult enough, I didn't have that killer gaze, I wasn't good enough to have a child with him, not up to snuff, not whole enough, I suddenly felt like a caterpillar who's failed the butterfly exam.

It was after the abortion that he began going out more and more often without me, to parties, weddings, nightclubs, dinners I stopped going to because I thought I'd say the wrong thing, silly things that I didn't think important but that he'd tell me later, his face white with rage, his jaws clenched, that they had humiliated him, dishonored him, that they had ruined his political career.

It was during those sad evenings when I finally preferred staying home with the cats, smoking cigarettes and playing with my computer and thinking of the time when he wouldn't even ask me to go with him anymore, when he would stop insisting, even for form's sake, and when he'd meet a girl who was more beautiful, more amusing, more warlike, with more of a killer gaze, that's when everything started and I became this drug addict.

First I went to see Mom's homeopath.

"Do you always talk so fast?" he asked me.

"Yes, I think so."

"Why?"

"From fear."

"Fear of what?"

"Of boring people too much, I think."

"Do you feel depressed?"

"No. Just floating. Sometimes in the air, sometimes in very deep water. There's an emptiness inside me. It's like helium, it carries me far away from people, far away from things, but that's not the problem."

"What is the problem?"

"I think I'd like to be someone else, sometimes."

"Who?"

"Anyone. A Superwoman with a killer look, for instance."

"Why?"

"Because of Adrien. My husband, Adrien. He thinks I'm not the right woman for him. I sleep too much, for instance. Sometimes I sleep fifteen hours a lay, sorry a day, and in my dreams I'm someone else, someone who's much more pleasing to him."

He said yes I understand, he asked me if I like vinegar, yes a lot, and chocolate? that too, and he prescribed a treatment for me. The first medication was called cocainum, that made me laugh. The second was cocculus, I didn't like that so much. But neither of them did anything for me. They did nothing to change this emptiness in me. I still felt just as ill, just as caught up in fatigue, a thick fatigue that covered everything, that sleep didn't lessen. What's more, I was making just as many gaffes as before. I still couldn't manage to take an interest in Adrien's career, in the conferences he was organizing along with super-ancient ministers, in the notes he wrote to them, in the evenings when he went out to flatter them, in all his complicated strategies I was too silly to go along with. And that's how one day, when I was looking for something in my father's office desk, I came across his brain pills.

I knew he took them, sometimes, to work, to stay awake, to finish his books. I knew it made him nervous, concentrated, short-tempered, quick. I had always known they were there, in the cave of Ali-Papa. But it hadn't interested me any more than that. I passed over them without seeing them. He himself never talked about them, except with his writer friends when they were exchanging recipes and dosages. But now, I said to myself this is great, maybe this is the solution, I just need to keep them with me, everywhere, all the time, these little magic pills, and, first of all, I'll be brilliant, clever, fascinating, and, secondly, it will be a little of Dad in me, it will be as if he was with me, there will be two of us, two must be better than one, it will help me be up to snuff, that's just what I need to be worthy of Adrien.

That's how it all began.

Once, twice, then more and more often, every day, every hour, eight to ten a day, whenever I doubted myself, whenever I felt Adrien's reproachful look and I wanted to recover quickly, whenever I panicked and wanted to call for help: Upsy-daisy, Dad in my pocket, direct access to Dad's cortex, everything became easy, fluid, almost clear, I felt I was cured, invulnerable, Superwoman, I felt lighter, whenever I took it and until the next time I took it, I felt as if my bad habits, my escapes and renunciations, my fragility, my laziness and cowardliness, had all been removed. I felt freed of this cluelessness that so annoyed Adrien, freed of this emptiness I felt inside me that sucked everything up, my will, my desires, my happiness—capable, finally, of being the woman he wanted, the woman I wasn't.

These miracle pills were called Dinintel, or Survector, or Captagon, all you have to say is amphetamines, just amphetamines, since all these pieces of junk are the same, they all have the same effect. Amphetamines were what I needed. Amphetamines were what I was lacking, what I needed to be worthy of my husband, worthy of having a child with him, a child who would have had my Breton skin and his knobby knuckles, and I'd be worthy of appearing at his side during his political dinners, capable of not making gaffes in front of his Ecole Normale friends, capable of not being afraid anymore that he'd deceive me, leave me, fall out of love with me, abandon me, now there was no more danger, I was invulnerable, I was as strong as the Terminator.

I can still recall those feelings from back then, those wonderful, miraculous impressions, that vague feeling of being on a flying carpet, out of reach, triumphant.

But I also remember it was as if Dad was inside me, with me, in my head; nothing else could happen to me; like him, I didn't have to follow the dotted lines, I could jaywalk without looking; when I spoke, he was dictating; taking his amphetamines was like a transfusion, it was my life woven into his, it was something of his intelligence and his courage that passed into me; he was guiding me, protecting me, watching over me without knowing it, Adrien wouldn't abandon me anymore, I was finally the Superlouise Adrien dreamt of.

I knew nothing, then, about the nightmare to come, the depression, the pulmonary edema I almost died of, the hair falling out in tufts, the repeated illnesses, the increasing difficulty in running and even sometimes walking, I knew nothing about any of that, and, even if I had known, it wouldn't have changed anything, I would have kept going to the end, almost to the end, just as I did.

Anyway it's not true, I know that, I had so many doctors, and so many pharmacists, but still there was one, one doctor who was more important than the other ones, he looked after a great writer who was much more of a drug addict than I was, and right away he told me about the horrors that awaited me, he told me everything actually, but just like that, just to get it over with, basically he couldn't care less, he prescribed whatever I wanted, he even said to me one day, calmly, as he held out my second prescription of the week, you know, Miss, a doctor has never been able to prevent anyone from killing himself. When it was all over Dad went over and bashed his face in, he never dared complain, the asshole.

But I'm exaggerating when I say that, he wasn't the asshole, he wasn't the guilty monster, it was me, just me, I didn't care about increasing the doses all the time; I didn't care I'd stopped swimming and dancing because my heart couldn't stand it; I didn't care about dying. I didn't care about the waxy complexion I was beginning to get some mornings, big dark wrinkles I had to hide beneath thick layers of makeup; I didn't care about this hard, black look that betrayed me when I wasn't paying attention; I didn't care about the meanness I had inside me that the amphetamines revealed; I didn't care about being alone, more alone than I had ever been; I didn't care about anything, from the instant I had my twelve gel caplets per day and could say to myself: That's it, now I'm like the girl Adrien's looking for, that implacable being who always has an answer ready, my mind always glowing, feverish, never dreamy again. I didn't care that the world was hard, coarse, full of rough edges that caught on me like brambles, so long as I could get through them; I didn't care about becoming hard myself, and mean, so long as I was lucid, and clever, as he wished. It's a miracle, I told myself; this is how he loves me, disguised as Superlouise who sees through people right down to their guts, their vices, their evil thoughts, their flaws, and that's how I can exist, if I want, when I want, thanks to speed; the gentleness of childhood was far away; the time when I laughed when I heard Dad say to a friend on the phone so then, my dear super-cube, he said dear super-cube and I heard dear Rubik's Cube, I was in seventh heaven; all that was far away but actually things seemed close, I could understand the codes and the trends, amphetamines allowed me to see and hear, they were the whole world right in my face, like the first time they put glasses on me, amphetamines were the key to everything, thanks to amphetamines I was worthy of being loved.

All that's very remote, now. Remote, and cold. It's all coming back again, as if from the bottom of an abyss. Because very soon the nightmare began.

twelve

I learned how to fake prescriptions, how to trick the doctors who in any case didn't much resist prescribing whatever I wanted. I just changed the quantities. I knew druggists who, for a little commission (they kept the money the insurance company paid, or else charged extra for other things), agreed to close their eyes to shady prescriptions. Quickly and completely I entered this other world where time is no longer the same, time is counted in tablets, in pills, in hours that were void or full, full of strength or hollowed out from bouts of nausea when I ran out or had taken too many.

Then, much later, when I really wanted to stop—but how could I, I would have had to be very strong to stop, but I wasn't strong at all, that's why I started this madness in the first place and knocked myself out with amphetamines—I remember those nights spent at home, vomiting, crying, unable to do anything but wait for my appointment with the next doctor who would renew my prescription, wait for a miracle, for the coffee to kick in, or for me to find a Dinintel under the bed, or for the ceiling to collapse and give me a real reason to be unhappy.

I remember that famous night of Adrien's birthday, I can't get up, I can't, it was to be good at these kinds of dinner parties, to be up to the mark, that I got into all this and now, six months later, my legs can't even support me anymore, I'm even more inadequate, even more useless, than when I wasn't taking anything, oh if I could only find a Captagon, just one, it's been a long time since it gave me the superpowers it did in the beginning, but at least I could get up, get washed, get dressed, make believe, go with him for at least an hour or two, time for the effect to wear off, but no, I stay in my bed, I let him go alone to this birthday party where all his friends will be along with supergirls who will goggle at him with their big fish-eyes, I remember because he was very angry at me, for a long time afterwards.

But how could he have gone on for so long not realizing anything was wrong, not getting worried, not calling my father, not calling for help, not doing anything? It's a mystery. He has a theory, today, about that. Adrien has always loved theories. He'd walk back and forth in front of me as if in front of a large audience, he'd stop in front of the mirror to replace a lock of hair that was falling in front of his eyes, or fiddle with a button, or verify the vehemence of his gaze, he'd scarcely look at me, as he explained his theory. His theory, today, is that... Oh! I don't really give a fuck about his theory. I think he just wanted not to see, not to know. I think he was like everyone else, I can't get angry at him, eaten away by his ambitions, his friends, their little baby-politician plots to take some association or some conference by storm. I think he also thought, deep down, that I was crazy, super-fragile, and that, speed or no, it would turn out badly in the end for us, isn't that what he said to Simon, his best friend at the time, when we were separating, Louise is done for, I know it, it's over, but I couldn't do anything else, I couldn't keep it from happening, and that's just what bothers me most in my leaving her. That was pretty puffed up of him, to start with this idea that his little bear was done for, that it was all over, written in the cards, and that it had no more effect on him than that. And then there's also, I should say, the fact that I lied like a pro, maybe I really put him off the scent, maybe he thought I was just a lazy hypochondriac whacko egotist. Why did I lie? Because, despite everything, despite the hell my life had become, I didn't want to stop. Because I didn't want to go back to the way I was before, nice little Louise who's afraid, who hides, who blushes. And also I lied because I was ashamed, whatever happened I didn't want him to know that I needed a crutch to be an adult, I was ashamed of the person I was when I was naked, without amphetamines, without my Superlouise disguise.

Plus without amphetamines I wasn't the same as I was before. It wasn't so simple, it wasn't enough for me just to stop, remove the disguise, to become little Louise again. No, when I stopped, I was a vegetable. I needed a superhuman courage to get up. I opened my eyes, I didn't see anything, I told myself I have to go to the bathroom, clean my contacts, take my first Dinintel, my Survector-Effexor-Incital cocktail, but even for that I couldn't be bothered, I went back to sleep, woke up again ten minutes later, in a sweat, in the middle of a terrible dream, I drank a little water, how did that dream end, how did it end and where was it heading, even for that I didn't have the strength, I didn't see anything, didn't hear anything, just Adrien, far away, talking on the telephone, or to the cats, or to his reflection on his watch, that woke me up a little, I grumbled, went to the bathroom to swallow my tablets, came back and sank into bed, closed my eyes, waited for the cocktail to start taking effect, what time is it? Eleven o'clock, and what if it doesn't work this time? If it has even less effect today than it did yesterday? Noon, that's good, it's a start, I feel the first effects, I have nothing interesting to do, I can go back to sleep, I go back to sleep, when I really emerge it's the middle of the afternoon, I'm in a bad mood, I'm furious, I shout I'm sick of it in the bathroom, the telephone rings, the answering machine sounds distorted, oh fuck, messages that were going to bawl me out, to make me feel guilty, I won't call anyone back, anyway people know by now that I don't return calls anymore, why don't they give up, if I were them I'd go out for a walk, I'd stop calling people. Get up, get dressed, go down and have a coffee at the counter at Danton, leave a message for Dad to say hello, it's Louise, no time to talk or see you, I'm working a lot, it's great, I needed a superhuman courage to be capable of doing that, I needed all my last remaining little strength to do anything else but wait for a lull with no nausea, fake the next day's prescription and go, thin and broken, to act out the comedy at the pharmacy.

"This prescription isn't at all clear." I hated this role I took on, this semi-crime I saw myself falling into, I hated sometimes having to beg, implore, beseech, why do they care, why are these pharmacists making it so difficult, what does it cost them? I hated the vigilant ones, the ones who checked and verified, who called their boss and discussed my prescription in whispers, while I tried to look both honestly and unhappily kind whereas I wanted to bite them. And I also detested the accomplices who, as time went by, thought we were friends and told me about their dogs their vacations their tai-chi classes, and I had to listen, and make comments, and laugh, I wanted to kill those girls. And then there were the ones who blackmailed me, they're the ones I understood best because at least they were playing the game, they knew they were risking being denounced to the pharmacists' association one day or another. I avoided the pharmacies where I used to dawdle before, trying on the latest sunscreens or asking advice for a hair conditioner, and the ones who asked me how my tonsillitis or my little brother's ear infection was, I was too ashamed, I felt I was no longer someone you'd associate with. Anyway, rumors travel fast, and those druggists didn't say hello to me anymore when I met them at the supermarket.

It's strange Adrien didn't leave me then. He didn't even leave me when he knew, when I confessed everything to him. He came into the living room, at three in the afternoon, and found me on the sofa, sick, in convulsions, and he just began screaming. Sometimes I'm grateful to him for that, I tell myself at least he stayed, he put up with my convalescences and my relapses, my lies and my hysterical scenes. Sometimes I tell myself he needed me to need him, that deep down, he liked this intermittent Saint Bernard role, taking me to the hospital, flirting with the nurses, playing out his own tragedy and mine too, taking on, in front of the doctors, his young-husband-who-is-so-to-be-pitied look. And then when he kept telling me over and over you have to kill the father! You have to kill the father! And I believed him just as I had believed him when he told me he was sterile, when he forced me to talk to my father furtively, or not to talk to him at all, I didn't know yet that actually, beyond his kindness, his goodness, he had this desire: He wanted to kill my father, and I was his weapon.

In the beginning I put him off the trail, I was very careful about everything, my gestures, my trembling, I simulated appetite, at table, like the others, and fatigue at night, after lovemaking that was a struggle, a fistfight, a gallop, fists clenched, teeth grinding. I got up while Adrien slept, I lifted weights in the living room to make myself tired but it didn't, I read books I don't have any memory of, I know I read them, the pages are dog-eared, annotated, some sentences are underlined, but I don't remember anything, all that for nothing, I had superpowers, I was Superlouise, but I didn't do anything at all except for the beginning of a pulmonary edema.

Oh yes, I remember that at night I was seized with a frenzy of tidying up and cleaning, I scoured the floor, disinfected the doorknobs, bustled about, rearranged my books and Adrien's, and then finally I felt the exquisite moment, close to orgasm, that moment when the five, six tablets of Stilnox or Rohypnol finally started working, gained the upper hand over the amphetamines, that moment when I felt I was sliding into sleep, that thick, dreamless sleep, that sleep like burning tar poured over my body, that buried everything, covered everything, I'd have given anything for that instant, for that nanosecond when I felt I was being switched off, like a computer. Adrien found me in the morning asleep, curled up in a ball on the living room sofa, rubber gloves on my hands and a bandana in my hair, he laughed, he said I was a sleepwalker, his little sleepwalking bear.

Do you love me? I asked in the rare, very rare moments when I rediscovered some of the reflexes of the old Louise. Yes my love, my little bear, I love you, but I'd like it better if you got up in the morning. Me too, I'd like that, can't you get me up in the morning? Can't you shake me? That's what I do, my little bear, but you grumble, you're delirious, you hit me, you say no, no, let me sleep, let me finish my dream, what do I have to do to get you up, I have appointments, I'm busy, I have my career, for Christ's sake. We didn't argue much, though. I was a lump of love or a lump of sleep, I didn't have much time to argue.

In the end I was taking the capsules in threes, fives, sevens. I was mixing them up. I was shortening the time between pills. Three Dinintels and two Survectors every three hours, just to be able to perform, mechanically, the daily gestures you usually do without thinking about it, standing up, showering, buying bread, meeting other people, all the other people who filled me with fear again, fear like before, before I was on drugs. For my aim, now, was just to cope, just be capable of pretending. But the superpower, the lucidity, the intelligence, my father in my head, all that was over, I didn't have access to that anymore, the amphetamines had opened up then closed the doors to the world and I was beginning, like before, to walk on tiptoe again, excusing myself, always thinking I'm bothering people, always afraid of saying stupid things, and always afraid that Adrien would leave me. The disguise was no longer disguising me, and without the disguise I didn't exist anymore at all. What is a mask if there's no one behind it?

thirteen

And then there was that Sunday just before I went into the clinic, in the restaurant I used to go to with Dad, except that, for a year now, I'd been canceling our meetings there more and more often with all kinds of excuses: Because I couldn't lie as well as I used to, because it was becoming increasingly difficult to simulate good health and the nice little Louise from before, because I wasn't getting up and also because Adrien made a scene whenever I told him I was going out to lunch with Dad and because I was too exhausted to put up with his fits, I preferred canceling again and telling Dad sorry, I'm busy, too bad, we'll meet after Christmas, after Easter, or maybe when Atlantis rises from the sea....

It's hard for him, of course. He can't understand
why his little Louise is becoming so distant. But at least
he doesn't know. He has no idea about what I'm
drowning in, because of me, through my fault alone,
because I wanted to do right, yes, I swear to you I
thought I was doing the right thing, it was so that you
could be proud of me, Dad, Mom, Grandma, Adrien
especially, really proud of your Louise, look how
happy she is, lively, alert, intelligent, look how she gets
up in the mornings in top form, how hard she works,
how talented she is, what a good little trooper, she's all
grown up now, she used to be so shy, so reserved, she's
gained so much confidence, it's unbelievable!

That Sunday, though, I came. I took a double dose
of Dinintel and Captagon to be sure I could be as
euphoric as I needed to be. I sat down with my back
to the room, in front of the mirror, so I could keep
checking on how I looked: Dad knows me by heart; he
knows me better than Adrien; and he knows the effects
of these fucking amphetamines too, he takes them from
time to time, to work fast, to finish an article or a
book, he takes them for two or three days, then he
stops, he's always had the strength to know when to
stop, now he doesn't take them anymore, I think I
turned him off of them, he told me maybe, in ten years,

when he's absolutely sure I'm completely cured; I am completely cured, is he entirely convinced of that?

But that day I can't go on. No use stuffing myself with chemicals, no use getting so high on Captagon that my temples are pounding, my heart is racing, I have pins and needles in my legs and arms, I have cramps, I've had it, I can't go on with this comedy and also I'm afraid, I'm more afraid than I ever remember being. Yesterday I heard that Dinintel was going to be banned from sale in pharmacies, and Captagon too, and all the amphetamines. What am I going to do, I wonder. How am I going to be able to do without them? Am I still capable of stopping? How? I wasn't so bad, really, before. Adrien really did fall in love with me, before. Why not try to become as I was before, just as I was, when I drank Coke, when I blushed, when I wasn't an addict, when he loved me?

Dad's in a good mood, I can see right away. He's happy to see me. He thinks I don't look well but he's happy to see me again. Do you know how long it's been? He asks me as he kisses me. Eight months! Eight months I've been deprived of my Louise! Me too, I'm happy, I'm always happy when I see him, but at the same time I want to cry and I have to make a super-human effort to make him think I'm normal, not to let

him notice anything's wrong, not to let him see I'm
drugged up to my ears, or that I can't go on and I'd
give anything, that day, to go back to square one.

He talks to me about Mexico, where he's going to
go to make a movie. He went there a long time ago
with Mom. It's a magical country, he says to me.
You'll see, you'll both see, you'll both come visit for
two or three weeks, you and your brother, you'll love
it. And as I'm listening I'm trying to calculate, as fast
as I can, the number of packages I'll need to get
through two or three weeks. Do they search the suitcases, in Mexico? I'll have my prescriptions, of course,
I won't risk anything. But if the customs inspectors
take out the boxes in front of everyone, and in front of
Dad... Just thinking about it, my heart is in my mouth
and I want to burst into tears.

Dad looks at me, as always, deep into my eyes.
Usually he guesses everything. He guesses and sees
everything. The sadness masked by a sore throat. The
little frown that means I'm worried. He suspected my
first cigarette, when I was fourteen, with Prune: We had
inhaled on the winding path that leads to the Marne, in
the house near Meaux where we used to spend the summer, before, in the blessed time of childhood, in the
blessed time of irresponsibility, hugs, scoldings, in the

blessed time of good habits. Prune had said to me, self-importantly, as she made smoke rings with her Gauloise, do you know your father has a new fiancée, my godfather told me, they say she's Mexican, and blond, and she speaks five languages, and she knows how to sing and dance, and she's ten years younger than him, and they're really in love, she's so perfect it's enough to make you want to shoot yourself, she has legs like this, and eyes like that, she's going to spoil our adolescence! I knew this new fiancée already. Dad had just introduced her to me. And right away I felt we'd become friends and that she might be my salvation. But it annoyed me so much that Prune knew it too and was showing off that I instantly decided not to see her anymore and since, in the meantime, I had taken her cigarette, I wanted to make smoke rings like hers and I began coughing like crazy. When it came time for dinner, Dad took my hand kindly in his. I instinctively withdrew it, because it was the hand that had held the cigarette and even though I'd washed it off with soap it was the hand at fault, the guilty hand. And, in my gesture, right away, he saw everything and understood everything: Louise, have you been smoking? Why did you do that? Don't you know how ugly that is? And stupid? It's not very sexy, you know, when women smoke and get plastered.

But that's not what I'm thinking about, that day, as I let him look at me, like before, right in my eyes. I'm thinking this lunch is my one last chance. I'm telling myself it's my only chance to let him see, for once, the little pinheads that are giving me such a hardened look. I tell myself that he has to understand. Yes, a complete change in strategy, he has to understand, he has to get angry, he has to help me, Dad always sets everything right he used to say to me, before, when everything was reparable, he's the only one who can set everything right, doctors can't do anything, doctors prescribe whatever I want and don't give a damn, and as to Adrien, it's too remote from him, he doesn't give a damn either, and also he's still a child, he doesn't understand anything very well, he'd tell me you have to talk to your father about it, so here we are, I'll stall for time, I'll try to make my father understand and he'll arrange everything, the way only he can do.

Help me, Dad, I say silently, fixing my hard eyes in his, my drug-fiend's eyes in his kind father's eyes. Help me, I murmur, help me, you're the only one who can get me out of this mess that was supposed to bring us closer together and that has put so much distance between us that I can't even talk to you anymore and it's been a year now that I haven't even seen you, and two years that I've been avoiding your gaze, because, for those two years when you just thought I was distancing myself because that's the nature of things, because children grow up, fall in love and forget their parents, I was in love, but with a boy for whom I wasn't enough, a boy who loves me, I think, but who wants me to be someone else, or for me to be everyone else, I wasn't distancing myself, I was running away, I was scared to death you'd see through me, you'd know, but now look, I've just changed my mind, you have to know now, you absolutely have to, from the bottom of my eyes I'm crying out to you, it's me, Louise, help me, I'm locked in, you're the only one who can help me, save me, tear me away from all that, you understand everything, you can fix everything, I'm a liar up to my neck, I'm lying to you as I've never lied to you before, I used to lie for little things, things so little you had to use all your powers of detection to confuse me, I'd give so much to go back to those kinds of lies, those normal unimportant lies, those lies all children use with all parents, there's a strike at school, I'm not the one who ate the chocolate, I'm sleeping over at my friend Delphine's, no I don't know where your grey cashmere sweater is, what about this new cat, I don't know, no, I'm not the one who brought it home: It's my entire life that's a lie now, in the afternoon when I wake up, in the morning when I go to sleep, it's no longer me, it's a lie of me, I can't bear to be this lie anymore, I want to go back, I'm begging you, I can't bear it anymore.

And then something extraordinary happens. Dad doesn't understand. Dad, who understands everything, looks at me but doesn't understand. It's too weird, probably. It's too remote. And I have such a habit of dissimulation that I'm probably continuing to lie even when I'm shouting out the truth. You look tired, is all he says to me. Are you working too hard? And I want to burst out in tears, right there, right in the middle of the meal I haven't touched. If I burst out in tears, he'll ask me what's wrong, if he asks me what's wrong he'll be prepared for a confession, there, that's what I have to do, that's exactly what I'll do and the nightmare will stop. And then another extraordinary phenomenon, another catastrophe, this one worse than before: Another little voice rises up in me, come from my innermost depths, a little voice that should have been stifled by the amphetamines and that whispers to me that Dad is so happy, there, facing me, so happy with his Mexico, so proud of my little brother and so proud of my first novel, so proud of me who've been so drugged for two years, that will hurt him so much, it will be such a shock to him, I owe him so much, I love him so much, I've caused so much anxiety for him already, does he deserve this, this unworthy daughter, this invalid? So I gulp down my sob, I change it into a sneeze, I say I have some dust in my eye, I say yes, I am a little tired, I smile at him, and, in my smile, I put all my kindness, all my sincerity, all that's left of my childhood, I give him my good model child's smile.

The waiter comes and serves the coffee. I feel the package of Dinintel in my pocket. Delicately, with my thumbnail, I detach a capsule, then another, then another. Dad asks if there's any pistachio ice cream. He raises his head towards the waiter, upsy-daisy, that's just enough, the capsules are in my mouth, under my tongue, I wait a little bit, not too long or the powder will come out of the gelatin capsule and the horrible taste will make me grimace. I smile. I was already smiling, but I change my smile which must have become fixed. I take my glass, firmly, so as not to tremble. I swallow a mouthful of Coke, then another. In ten minutes I'll feel better. For an hour, maybe a little more, I'll feel better. For an hour, maybe a little more, I'll play the comedy of cheerfulness, vivacity, happiness. Dad will be happy. He'll think I'm in good form, a real little success story, a dream of a young

woman, he'll tell me I still have the same forehead I
had when I was a baby, we'll talk about all the important things, as usual, as before, about my brother who
wants to be a lawyer, about my grandmother who's
taking computer classes, about Adrien's kindness, and
we'll leave the restaurant before the first onset of nausea. Anyway it's over, I feel better already, oh my God,
what a crazy idea, what a mistake that would have
been, that was a close call, I'll get along fine all by
myself in the end.

fourteen

It was Adrien who dropped me off at the clinic, in a taxi, with a suitcase full of books and two nightgowns.

Pretty grounds, strict but reassuring nurses, people in tracksuits in the hallways, small austere bedroom, it was a far cry from *One Flew Over the Cuckoo's Nest* and, even if it wasn't Club Med, I thought the place was all right, I was ready to stay there for a year if I had to, or two, or more, I'd be able to read my heart out, sleep without hiding, not have to pretend to be cheerful, cry non-stop since here you have the right, this kind of place must even be made for that, a place where you can really cry in peace.

I said quick go away my love my angel, I was in such a hurry to cry, I was so impatient to see what it

was like not having to control your face, your emotions, how you look, go away, you'll miss your bus,
darling, and I went to sit down in the big common
room to meet my new friends, the ones I'd play foosball with, the ones from the occupational therapy
workshop, the ones who had been raped, who had
arrived with their gums destroyed by injections, who
weren't there of their own free will and drank 90 proof
alcohol neat, who were even more addicted to drugs
than I was, who were depressed, alcoholic, elec-
troshocked, the aggravated schizophrenics, the others,
the many others, the ones who could no longer say why
they were here because they had forgotten, they've been
here for years.

Every night, at 10 PM, they gave me my dose of
Tranxene. I prefer Urbanyl, mixed with Lysanxia, that
gets me higher, but they insisted on Tranxene and I
didn't dare protest. In the morning, at 9 AM, knock
knock, good morning, breakfast, here's your Effexor,
wait I don't have my contacts, that's okay, open your
mouth. At noon, bon appétit, here's your Buspar, no,
take it in front of me please. The rest of the time, crying I strung beads in the occupational therapy workshop, weeping I played foosball, moaning I read *Fraulein
Else*, I watched "The X-Files" in the bed of a handsome

boy with a stomach lacerated by knife cuts whom I liked a lot, who also cried a lot and never spoke.

He had big rather empty very blue eyes, eyes like mirrors in which you saw whatever you wanted: the sky, or nothing at all. He had finished his course of treatment, but he didn't want to go home. He reminded me of my Uncle Pierre, my mother's brother, who hasn't left his house in ten years, they bring him food every morning, he sleeps, he eats, he sleeps, he eats, occasionally he gets dressed, he puts on his handsome blazer with gold buttons from when he was rich daddy's boy from Rennes with a convertible, gorgeous girls, brilliant life, long carefree afternoons on the terrace of the Café de la Paix, but he can't manage to make up his mind, crossing the threshold of his apartment is an unbearable suffering for him and, finally, he doesn't go out, takes off his blazer and goes back to bed for the week. This boy was the same. He took root there for a year and they ended up having to throw him out. We were surprised, one day, by a nurse who told on us to the head doctor and they put us on different floors.

Dad came to see me. He spread panic, the first time, in the lobby, with his dark glasses and his rock-star look, in the middle of patients in tracksuits and my new zombie friends. He told me I was much prettier like this, fragile, a little shy, that's how he loved me, that's how I would be happy, for I was going to be happy he knew that, you'll see I'm right he said, you'll see I'm never wrong, have I ever been wrong? No, no, Dad, I replied, you're never wrong. I wanted so much to believe him. And I wanted so much, too, to reassure him, to make him understand there was nothing rotten in me, nothing spoiled or decayed, that I was still his little Louise, the surface just needed a little cleaning, that's all, just a little tidying up. We went to the park and took long walks together. He took me out to lunch in the local inns. He brought me books, newspapers. Since if you pretend you feel a certain way for long enough you really do, it ended up almost working and, by dint of acting the model child, I rediscovered almost normal reflexes. I began to read again. I listened to my brother's news. I felt I was returning from a long journey, from a country very, very far away, I was like the man with the broken ear in that old Edmond About story who was frozen for I don't know how many years and who comes to in a completely unfamiliar world.

My grandmother also came to see me. My little grandmother who's gone now, but she's the one who had found the clinic, she's the one who had organized everything with that nice doctor who was completely depressive but reassuring. I usually hate people who say "gone" instead of "dead." Gone where, you wonder. It's stupid, it's ridiculous, the way people have of pussy-footing around, of not saying anything openly, like saying "Israeli" so the word "Jew" doesn't burn your tongue. Well now I've become like that—I'm talking like all the other idiots. I say "gone" too. But it's so hard for me to say it. I didn't cry the day of her funeral but the more time passes the sadder I am that she's gone and the more I see her again, those weeks, at my bedside, laughing and serious as she used to be, reassuring, posi-tive, she's the one who saved me, finally.

Her name was Dinah, I always said Granny because Mommy was already taken, but still there were times when I slipped up—did I slip up or did I just pretend to—I called her Mommy, no, sorry, Granny, I was five years old, I laughed at my mistake, that was when she went with me to the hotel where Dad lived and I'd say to her goodbye Mommy, no, Granny, and I'd burst out laughing and couldn't stop.

Her name was Dinah, there are so many things I'll never laugh at again because of her, there are so many things I could do only with her and that I'll never do again without her: I'll never ski again, I'll never swim to the tip of the cape at Antibes, I'll never take pictures

again, I'll never listen to Ella Fitzgerald or Dizzy
Gillespie again, you were the only grandmother in the
world with whom you could suntan bare-breasted, you
went swimming all year long in your pool, in the winter it was 60 degrees out and you still went swimming,
I'd stay on the edge of the pool, with my slice of bread
and Nutella, counting your kicks, at a hundred I'd
shout Stop and felt useful, I was glad to be useful. And
then that bitter almond inside the apricot kernel we
were both crazy about, you'd say it's supposed to be
poisonous but if it was poisonous I'd have died fifty
years ago, you weren't afraid of poison, you thought
you were immune to death, when you left for the
Amazon you didn't want to take Nivaquine because
you thought you were stronger than malaria, you
caught it anyway and you cured yourself of it, when
I'm sick I crumble to pieces.

You weren't afraid of anything, really, and then
you got that horrible cancer usually only men get, I
was furious at the doctors, I had to get furious at
someone, you never smoked in all your life, you were
so young, so healthy, until I was fifteen I actually
thought you were thirty-seven, yes, you must be thirty-
seven, you'd never change, and that was okay if it was
almost Dad's age, that's how it was, it was your age

for life, like your first name or the color of your eyes, is that your grandmother? She looks so young, how old is she? Thirty-seven, I replied, and they must have thought I was crazy. You came every day. You took me out for strawberry milk at the Sofitel at the end of the avenue leading to the clinic. You brought me the latest episode of "General Hospital" that we watched on the VCR. You took good care of me and with you too I acted the good child.

Adrien came the first weekend. I hadn't realized it was already the weekend, time passed without passing, it was like one single day, or one single night, one night full of cramps and retching, I was sick as a dog. He came unannounced, with some chocolate, cigarettes, an ashtray, some grass, a framed photo of him, a photo of us he thought he looked good in, incense paper. Thank you, thank you, I said to him as he unwrapped his gifts. Thank you, that makes me so happy. But I gathered all my little strength and ran like Speedy Gonzalez into the bathroom to make myself up: mascara, powder, damn, that definitely emphasizes my wrinkles, put on some foundation, how could I have forgotten foundation? I begin crying, all alone, in front of the mirror while he starts talking to me, through the closed door, about a dinner of Important People that's coming up next Sunday, he'd like me to come just this once, do I think that might be possible? Do I think I'll be cured by then? And can I promise not to make any of my usual gaffes that always botch up his whole career? No, no, I shout, I won't make any gaffes; yes, yes, I'll be cured, I'll come; good God, does he still not have a clue? Has he not grasped the fact that I almost had an embolism, I'm there for weeks, maybe months? Damn, now my mascara's running! What a stupid idea, anyway, putting on mascara in my state! I rub my eyes, notice a horrible pillow crease streaking my cheek, rub that too, that makes the powder come off, I put another massive dose on, now that makes big bags, those are even worse, and the pillow crease is still there, if he sees me like that he'll leave me, already I probably can't go to any more of his dinners, if he sees me with this face on top of that I'm fucked, fortunately I find my pair of sunglasses, they're not big but at least they'll hide my red eyes, I gather my breath, compose a calm, serene look, put my hair in front to hide most of my face and leave the bathroom.

I'm happy to see him, of course, but a little panicked too, what will we talk about? I'm not up on anything that's going on now. I haven't been interested in anything for months. The slightest emotion makes me break out into tears and I know he hates it when I cry, he always takes that as an insult to him, why are you doing this to me, he says to me when I'm upset, why are you doing this to me? And also the five minutes of preparations have exhausted me, my head's spinning, everything's getting muddled up in my mind, and I stretch out on the bed. He's fortunately standing by the window, not looking at me. He'll stay like that for an hour, standing up, and I think that, during that hour, he didn't look at me one time: I might as well not have made myself up, I could have had snot on my nose and been wearing hideous thick glasses! What are we going to say to each other, I wonder. How can I reassure him a little? I'm so worried and so much in a daze at the same time that I want him to go away soon: If I'd had a Dinintel, I think that I'd have swallowed the whole bubble pack just for that.

Not him. I'm happy to see you, he says, I missed you so much, I'm not doing well, my little bear, I needed for us to talk and for you to comfort me. Thank you, I repeat, thank you. And he begins to talk, talk, I even begin to wonder if he hasn't taken speed too, but no, at a certain point when he leaves his window to see if his cell phone is on, I see his pupils, they're not too dilated, he's just excited, maybe deep down he likes the situation, he doesn't know what to concentrate on, he says one thing and then its opposite, there's no sense in regretting things but we should have kept the baby, he wants to stop smoking but that would be like leaving me, he's unhappy with his life and he loves life, I look exactly like my cat but he prefers dogs, he's going to write a novel, put some money aside, take the teacher's exam again, re-read *Adolphe*, he's so like Adolphe. I say: No! really? what a good idea! wow are you sure? and he keeps going, he walks back and forth in the little bedroom as he used to do when he told me his theories at home, he drags frantically on his cigarette, runs his hand through his hair, looks at himself in his watchface, and starts up again better than before, why he hesitates between Marxism and ultra-liberalism, his infallible painful memory, his memories that are poisoning him, his sadness, his melancholy, it's devouring me do you understand, it's consuming me, nothing is impossible for an intelligent person, France is definitely a boring country, he likes seeing me so peaceful but he feels alone, so alone, he's going to die he's so alone.

I'm here, I say to him, impressed all the same to see him with tears in his eyes, and moved, and wanting to pull him towards me if I didn't have these bags of powder under my eyes and this lead hanging from my arms,

I'm here, I'll come home soon, and now I'm the one feeling a wish to cry rising up, since I can see, as I say them, that those are exactly the same words Mom had said to me, just ten years ago, during her own detox treatment. But Adrien doesn't hear, he doesn't notice I'm crying, he's still not looking at me, or he's looking at me without seeing me, I could be shooting heroine, or sniffing glue, or dead, or sticking out my tongue at him, he just needs a witness, I'm there, nailed to the bed, that's convenient, so he gets even more worked up, he explains he hates neurotic environments, he's sad too but at least he knows why, should I take that personally? Should I answer and tell him I know why I'm sad, that I'm sad for imposing all this on him, this visit to the clinic, this crazy life, these days spent sleeping, these nights trying to sleep, these fits of hysterics, these scenes of jealousy? But I can't find the right words, everything gets mixed up in my head, the ideas die one after the other, my mouth is dry and finally I understand that it's not a question of me but of him, of him alone, and also of his father, of the mystery that links them together, of their lives that are so alike, of their intelligence their passion, so I let him soliloquize, it seems to be doing him good, I'm the one who's sick but he's the one who needs to be listened to.

He says again that insomnia is wearing him out, he has to stay true to the Cartesian principle of comprehension of reality, the curtains in the living room need changing, he's sick of traveling second class, could I peel him an orange, what effect do I think he's having on the nurses, he'll go see the doctor in any case, he'll say to him my wife, I want to know exactly what medication you're giving my wife. After a while, I stop listening. A word, a phrase, reaches me from time to time: neurasthenically active... great guy... conquer the universe... Jackie Chan... devour the world... slice through the armor... Swann Odette Charlus Agathe Godard... dirty fingernails... love each other when nothing prevents us... hyperbolic doubt... guilty desire... bitter taste in my mouth... I decide to pretend I've fallen asleep and when I wake up he's not there anymore, it's night, he's left, he left me a little note on the bed, nice little note, full of love, a little note that finally made me want to kiss him, a little note so like it was when we could talk to each other, when we understood each other, when I wasn't an addict yet and he wasn't so vain.

The next weekend, though, I asked him not to come back. I used the excuse of a raging flu, a virus that had contaminated the whole floor. That's okay, I had the flu shot! Yes but still, this flu is terrible, my roommate caught it despite the shot, if I were you I'd wait till next weekend, it'll be better then. He came back from time to time. The whole thing lasted four months. I needed all that time to become new again, so that I wouldn't need anything to get up or go to sleep, for my body to get strong, for it to become stronger than the me who was afraid, afraid of confronting the world without a crutch, afraid of my newly rediscovered health, afraid of starting up again, and he came during those four months, kindly, whenever he had a Saturday free. That's when I understood that something had become undone between us, that there was no more "between us," that nothing would ever be the same again. That's when I understood that my sickness was also called Adrien.

fifteen

What did you expect? I said to him. Did you think it would be easy to leave me? You think I'll let you go just like that? I threw the frame on the ground, the glass broke but since that wasn't enough I leaped out of bed and tore the photo apart, the one he claimed to like so much, the photo of us as newlyweds, beautiful and slightly ridiculous, there were so many people we didn't know at our wedding that we left before it was over.

He looked sad, more from the destroyed photo than from the fact of leaving me. He's always been crazy about photos. Sometimes I told myself that he liked real things just so he could see them in a photo some-day. I'm the opposite, nothing scares me more than a photo, nothing seems more two-faced to me than a beautiful photo of happiness with all the unhappiness it promises and contains, without saying so, carefully concealing its hand. I didn't know yet it was the best thing that could be happening to me, his leaving me. How could I know? He was my whole life, without him I didn't exist.

He was wearing new sneakers, that night. He was stretched out on the bed, his new sneakers on his feet. First I thought it was because he was happy with them, because he wanted to admire them and have me admire them, I didn't know that he was wearing them to leave, on the run, forever. Why don't you take your sneakers off? I asked. They're great, but it's two in the morning, you don't want to make love with your sneakers on do you my love? No, he said, not laughing or smiling, no, I don't want to make love with my sneakers on, I have something to say to you. Okay, what? I curled up against him. As I was coming home from my office, I had called him up: Do you need anything? No. Cheese, Frosted Flakes? No. Because I'm going shopping, we don't have any more Coke, or tea I think, don't you need anything? Nothing. You're sure, nothing, that's too bad, since I wanted to get you something nice, to please you. Then please, don't bring me anything if you want to make me happy. This conversation had stunned me. He usually never said no to Frosted Flakes. Or to cheese. Sometimes we got up at night, me to go drink a glass of milk, him to make himself a sandwich, we were together in the kitchen, sleepy, hungry, it was one of the times I liked the most, when his hair was messy, and he was naked in the cold, France Info on in the background so he could hear the results of the soccer game. But now he didn't want any cheese, nothing, that was the first time ever, it was weird.

Do you remember how we used to make fun of people who said Listen we have to talk? he said to me, lying on the bed, his new sneakers on his feet. Yes, why? Because now we have to talk, it's stupid but we have to talk. His chin was trembling, he looked like he does when he gets a bad grade, or like when he's argued with his father, or.... No, actually, his chin has never trembled like that, he's never looked like this, and I ask him, very softly, on the verge of tears, scarcely daring to ask the question, and not daring to hear the answer: We have to talk, but what about? And, since he's hesitating: Go on, go on, say it, I shout, suddenly standing next to him. I've just understood, in fact, and I hate him for that: Say it! Say it! Last week... he coughs, takes out a cigarette, looks for a light, can't find one, puts the cigarette down... last week, you were wearing your green dress, you know, the one that makes people turn around in the street and that always makes me so proud, you said to me that's it, I'm cured, I'm happy, I'm so happy we'll finally be able to really love each other, I'm not afraid anymore that you'll leave me, do you remember? Of course I remember: I felt so strong, that day, I had been off amphetamines for a year, I had stopped reading his diary, I didn't talk anymore in my sleep, and it's true I wasn't afraid anymore that he'd leave me, and it's true it was a funny kind of good news, it meant life was going to be lighter, lightness is so important. But I don't reply. I'm too shattered by what I'm beginning to understand and he's the one who goes on: Well I'm leaving, that's it, I'm leaving, that's the thing I wanted to say to you.

Why, why? I want to ask him. But I don't ask anything at all, I can't utter a word. And that's when I leap out of bed and fling the photo down, usually I'm the one who leaves him, he runs after me in the street, that's the game, we fight, fists flying, kicks, we're all bashed up, full of bruises, bumps, but that's the game, I leave so he'll say don't leave, but this isn't a game anymore, I have no desire to hit him, neither does he, and when I sit back down on the bed, arms hanging down, beside myself, he even tries to be kind, to stroke my hair a little, and I just look him in the eyes, without understanding: Leave, but leave where, why, it's so strange. Adrien left without my understanding, he left, that's all.

I think Adrien is a good person, despite everything. Despite everything, despite him, despite everything I'm telling everyone, I think he is someone who is kind and good. A good person, this guy who keeps phoning me, who wants to talk to me to explain things to me, who left but who wants me to be still there, at the other end of the line or the leash, and who wants me to keep thinking about him. A good guy, this strutting peacock who comes to see me at my office just to see the effect he makes, if heads will turn towards him, if my girlfriends will say oh! Adrien is so this, Adrien is so that, no one's more interesting than Adrien.... We had a game, before. He had to walk in front of a mirror without looking at himself. He never managed it. That made us laugh. I don't know if he can do that, now. Maybe not. But I wonder who gets to laugh at him now.

Plus he's so weak. Such a little boy. I've grown up, I'm not such a child anymore, not really a woman, an ex-woman, maybe, but at least I've grown up, but not him, he hasn't changed, he did all of that out of childishness, not out of meanness, out of childishness, and that's why I think he's still a nice guy. Sometimes I tell myself he's destroyed everything, he's become the slave of this leech of a woman, he's fucked up his whole life, just to get the better of his father, just because he thought by doing this he'd be equal to his father, and to mine, and to that whole bunch of fathers with whom he's obsessed, who eat away at him. When he was little, he lifted weights like a madman, every day, thinking of the time when he'd be big enough and strong enough to bash his mother's second husband's face in. Here it's the same. He's gotten together with Paula the way he used to lift weights, just to show the big people he was as big as they were, that he could have a woman with a killer look too. And also he likes to impress people too much. He'd kill his father and his mother just for the pleasure of making an impression. He almost did that too, kill his father just to impress a witch who couldn't bear to see a father and son love each other so much. Poor Adrien. To fall into such a stupid trap.

But maybe they are happy. Maybe they really love each other. Does that hurt me, to imagine him happy, far away from me, with her? Not even. Not anymore. I almost wish it did. Because it's such a drag when he comes to talk to me about his life, his moods, it's like he's looking for some stepping-stones from his unhappiness to my unhappiness. But I don't want any part of that. So he continues to be a part of the past. He talks to me about our past as if it were my future, thinking he'll move me and, when he sees I couldn't care less, that annoys him, it makes him crazy, he closes his little fists or acts all upset and that annoys me even more. I don't feel like I'm divorced, I feel like I'm a widow, a widow of this man who didn't want the child we'd made together. That's not the baby he wanted. I'm not the one he wanted it with. He said to me my little bear, you are my little bear, but he didn't want this child, we made it together and together we killed it, everything we made together is dead. Either he left with everything in me that was his, or I'm the one who's thrown everything out, I'm an empty envelope, I've become an empty envelope. In either case, there's nothing left.

That's not true, there are cigarettes. It's thanks to him that I smoke. I'm so happy. I love smoking. In the beginning, I smoked so I could put up with his cigarettes. Especially the last one, which disgusted me, he liked smoking one last cigarette in bed before he went to sleep and the smell of the cold tobacco in his hair, in the sheets, in our kisses kept me from sleeping, with the bed like a big ashtray, now it doesn't bother me, it's Pablo it bothers, but it doesn't disgust him enough for him to really start smoking, he just smokes when he's angry, it's better that way. I said to myself it's like you do for garlic, both of you have to eat it, Adrien smokes, I smoke.

In the beginning I didn't inhale the smoke, I looked like a copycat with my cigarette between my index and middle fingers—in my left hand of course so that, Mom told me, your right hand always smells good in case someone kisses your hand. She has these kinds of ideas, Mom does. That must have been done, hand-kissing, at her parents' place, in their old life, when they were young Breton country squires, distinguished, a little F. Scott Fitzgerald around the edges, before they too flipped their lid, mad, human wrecks, her and her lovers, him an eccentric old man. For my wedding, to which, of course, he was invited, he had sent me a letter: Madame, I do not have the honor of knowing you. In fact we had spent all our summers together, traveling in his trailer. Not her, she remained amusing till the end: I remember that postcard I found one day when I was going through her night table, the mass-produced kind, her photo was stapled to the card, there was a nice big head-shot of a real-estate developer and he wrote to her: You are the only aristocrat who can get away with wearing black lace underwear.

Dad said, when I was little, your maternal grandparents were followers of Charles Maurras, now
they've become the last hippies. My hippie granddad
got angry, or pretended to get angry, retorting he
wasn't a hippie but a doctor. Yes you are a hippie. But
no, Louise, no, and he explained the medicine of the
right and the medicine of the left to me, how he was
against social security because the poor had to be taken
care of for free, and that was up to the doctors to do,
not the government, haven't you read your Céline?

In the beginning I didn't know how to smoke very
well, I looked too serious, which made our friends
laugh. I don't see these friends anymore. They were our
band of friends, it doesn't make any sense to see them
anymore without Adrien. They called me up. They
wrote to me. It's too stupid, they said. But I crossed
them out of my address book. And then I changed
address books. And then I changed lives, completely
changed lives and completely changed friends, aside
from Delphine, but Delphine is special, she's my childhood friend, I don't say hello to them when I meet them,
I end up not meeting them anymore at all anyway, or
else I meet them but I don't recognize them anymore.

I studied how other people's hands moved, the long-
time smokers, their nonchalance, their offhandedness.

I copied their movements in front of my mirror, not to round your lips out too much when you exhale the smoke, you shouldn't see anything, shouldn't hear anything, with a little training you'll just see smoke, they'll think I was born with a cigarette butt in my mouth. After a month I smoked like a madwoman, I could never do anything halfway, I lit each cigarette with the butt from the one before, I smoked in taxis, in movie theaters, at the doctor's, in planes with the cigarette hidden under my seat and my hand fanned out over it —just two or three puffs—I never got caught, at school, in my bed, in my bathtub, on my days off, at my grandmother's funeral. Smoking kills? Yeah. So does living. And sleeping too much, and not loving, and being all dried up inside, and holding back your tears, and knowing that Adrien is in this trap. The other day I read the story of a couple who made love in front of everyone in an English train compartment. No one said anything. When they had finished, though, and lit a cigarette, then people got angry and pulled the emergency cord. That's what we've come to. That's all I have left of him, cigarettes. What will I have left when I quit?

sixteen

The terrible thing now is that we have nothing more to say to each other. The other day, for instance. We saw each other by chance, in an overcrowded café, but that's okay, I didn't want you to look for another café, it's chance, we just have to sit there, near the door, in the draft, beneath the stairway people use to go to the bathroom, what would you like? A coffee, and you? A beer.

You say Paula and me, Paula's exes, me and Paula's exes. You say my son, my thesis, my new apartment, my future book, my broadcast on Radio X, those fucking paparazzi that mess everything up, they hunt us down, poison our life, I don't know what's keeping me from punching them in the face. And it's just words, little words round as drops of water, frozen over but not mean, words that have stopped having any effect on me, words from a life that isn't our own, drops from a life that doesn't even resemble a life, you bore me.

I'm bored, that day, Adrien. We haven't seen each other for so long, and I'm bored. You must not notice it, I say to myself. Or maybe you do, I don't know. Unsure, to be kind, I say oh really, oh good, oh wow. And you, you think I'm interested in all that and you elaborate on it even more, you get more and more excited, with your stories of the Minister of Such-and-Such and the actor Whatsit you're so proud of telling me you've become friends with thanks to Paula. You make me sad, all of a sudden. I think you're cute, childlike, very Adrien Deume-like in your joy at rubbing shoulders with the Important People we used to make fun of before. And these gestures too, these new gestures, this trick you have now of showing your teeth as you blow out your cigarette smoke. And this habit, too, of looking around you wide-eyed, where did you get this habit? Who did you steal it from? Give it back please, give it back quickly, we would have thought that was hilarious, before, if someone had done that in front of us. Oh well, that's not important either, there is no more us, we don't exist anymore, do whatever you like, keep your gestures and your affectations. You say to me:

"You are free...."

"What?"

I was thinking about your gestures. I was telling myself it's always the same, you know who people love, what they're impressed by, what kind of goldfish bowl they've fallen into, just from a gesture, a tiny little gesture, that they've picked up and that doesn't let them go. I was thinking about that. So I wasn't listening to you.

"I am free," you repeat. "We are free, you are free."

"Oh really?"

"Really. I was yours at twenty but I don't belong to you now, you were mine at twenty but you don't belong to me anymore."

"No..."

"No. You don't belong to your father either anymore, you don't belong to anyone."

Oh no, help! not that. You aren't going to start playing that old record again. Near the end, after the clinic and the detox, it had become an obsession, you talked to me about nothing but that, my father this, my father that, my relationships with my father, how I had to free myself from my father, how you were going to help me and how it was even a sort of mission that you gave yourself, you have always had a missionary side, Adrien, it's one of your kind qualities and now it was your mission, you acted as if God had put you in my life with the mission of separating me from my father. Oh God what am I getting into? I said to myself. Is it such a tragedy to love your father? Is he going to stop with his wicked little phrases, his trick questions, his acid hints that are supposed to confuse me, make me aware of my grave dependence? One night, we were watching *The Mother and the Whore* on TV. He thought the movie was stupid and overtalkative. I was fascinated. Suddenly he got up, turned off the set and stood in front of me with an evil look in his eye.

"I know why you like this movie," he said to me in the same aggressive tone he'd have used if I'd started taking drugs again or if I had thrown Doxa, his cat, out the window, "you like it because Léaud, in this movie, is the spitting image of your father."

"I don't know," I replied, "maybe, but that's no reason to have a fit, is it? What are you getting at?"

"You just like this movie because of your father, that's all, there, that's what I'm getting at and it seems to me a huge enough thing for you not to take on that innocent look."

I didn't know what to say. He was probably right, I might even have admitted it, but it didn't seem that serious to me, whereas for him it was like a crime. I shook my head, didn't say anything, and he left. When he came back, we didn't talk about it again, it was so serious.

Was it jealousy? In the beginning, of course, I thought so. I told myself he's just jealous of my relationship with my father. I thought it was stupid, there are lots of different kinds of love, there isn't just one that's worth more than another and there's nothing to get jealous about, I love my father the way all daughters in the world love their father, all right, maybe a little more, so what? Afterwards, I thought he was jealous, not of me, but of him, a macho thing, a guy-rivalry thing, life, success, recognition, all those things, I never really knew how important they were to Dad, but for Adrien that counted so much, he kept a permanent log, what had your father done at my age? And then what after that? And me and me and me? Today, I can't help but think that a boy who, out of all the billions of women there are on the planet, goes out and finds exactly the one who's with his own father, and steals her away from him, must have a real father problem.

You're looking at me, you're waiting for an answer, a reaction, or maybe not, you just uttered those words to see where and how they'd fall. Well, they fall on the ground. They fall flat. I could say to you no, I don't agree, I don't feel free, I don't want to be free anymore, being free terrifies me, being free of what, of betraying, of deceiving, of hurting, of being alone? But I don't want to. I don't pick the words up. I just look at you

with your nervous air and your funny gestures that
aren't like you anymore but you must be telling yourself they'll impress the customers who couldn't care less
about us, actually. It was amusing, before, arguing with
you. It was amusing when I loved everything about you,
you as a whole, your weaknesses, your faults, I loved
your faults too, and I liked it when we argued, I liked
being wrong with you, and right with you, and kissing
you, and interrupting you to say wow you have such
soft skin, and playing at being a baby, and playing at
being an adult, and putting a finger in your mouth as
you were talking to annoy you a little, touching your
teeth, pressing the tip of your nose, roughing you up, I
belonged to you, you belonged to me, you know we
were like that. Now, I don't want to anymore. I don't
even feel sad. I'd like to, but I can't, I think you're too
dull, almost laughable, and also I've become a solid
block of egoism now, nothing can slip between me and
me, neither sadness nor unhappiness, I don't let anything enter except for pleasure, yes, I have that capacity, to filter what reaches me, to choose, I've chosen not
to be sad, or something in me has chosen for me, I
don't know, I don't want to know, it doesn't interest
me. Why did I ask for a beer? I hate beer.

You go on, you keep talking, but all alone, into
your beard, you have a beard now, when we loved each

other, before, you just had a moustache and also, when you didn't shave after a week you had a tiny dense clump in the middle of a few scattered hairs, it made me burst out laughing and you laughed with me, pluck, I said as I pulled it, it makes a plucking noise, and I laughed, and you laughed with me, now you're talking into your beard, you're mumbling something else about my father, the letter you wrote to him, did I read it, your letter, do I want to read it, you're so proud of having written him this letter of insults that you want me to read it and you're surprised it doesn't seem to interest me, poor Adrien, why are you so angry with them, with our fathers?

"We're actually all alone, you see. Alone facing the vultures. Watch out for the vultures, Louise, the vultures with human faces."

I'm getting on your nerves. This time, I want to say: Stop I'm getting on your nerves. But even for that we're not close enough. I could insult you, before, since I could love you. But I'm not going to insult you, like that, cleanly, without the counterpart of love.

Once, I remember, at the very end, we were yelling at each other about the Muslim veil rule in high schools. Paula was already there. It was the intermediary period between your father and you. She was sleeping with your father at night, but she was seeing you during the

JUSTINE LÉVY

day, and you liked her so much, and I sensed that.
I controlled myself. But I watched you laughing with
her on the beach, or whispering things in her ear, I said
to myself she's the Terminator, he told me she wasn't a
woman but a Terminator, I'm not going to be jealous
of the Terminator. That day, we were arguing about
the veil. We disagreed so much and shouted so much, I
wanted so much to hate you and for you to reassure
me, I had slammed the door and gone sulking away to
the other end of the field. We were at Porquerolles. It
was summer. That day, strangely, you didn't come
looking for me, maybe because she was there, and you
were acting proud. Night fell. I saw you moving about
in the distance, in the kitchen, with her, and your father
who didn't suspect anything, and the others. You
looked very happy. You had completely forgotten me. I
was hungry. I was afraid. Asshole, asshole, I thought,
but I can't sleep out there, so I came back all alone,
sheepish and covered with mosquito bites.

You say to me and what about you? Me, what
about me? You're fighting a lot, I hope, with Pablo?
No, I say, not much. Oh good, because Paula and I
beat the hell out of each other all the time. Great, I say.
Look, I also say, trying to find something to say, I have
a new pair of jeans. And you say look, in a suddenly

panicked way, but I prefer that to your Important Person's affectations, I'm beginning to lose my hair. Show me? You show me, you lift up the hair that's falling over your eyes. It's true you're losing your hair a little, but how should I react to that? Before, when I knew you by heart, I knew I had to reassure you, lie to you, say to you no it's not true you're not losing your hair. It's like when you told me I'm trigonocephalic, touch here, can you feel it? My skull isn't round, it's bumpy, bumpy in three places, thank God I'm not bald, imagine that, I'd be a monster! That amused me, before, when we were children, and when we loved each other, and when you'd never be bald. But now? Well someday, now, you'll be bald, but first you'll be balding, how horrible, balding, a balding husband, thank God I don't love you anymore and you're not my husband anymore.

I don't know what to say to you. I say it's true, you're losing your hair a little but that looks good on you, it's pretty. You smile at me. Or maybe I'm not the one you're smiling at. You're smiling with a sad smile, and your eyes are creased, and lots of little wrinkles like crow's feet around your eyes. You have aged, you're twenty-seven years old and you've aged, I wouldn't have noticed it if we were living together, but today I notice it and that's how I understand we've really separated. You understand it too. Now, you've just understood it. And you smile at me, with that sad smile that isn't really meant for me. You're not posing, today. You didn't foresee this meeting, you haven't rehearsed and so you're not posing.

I try, as I look at you, to see you as you were before, with my eyes from before, when you weren't dead yet. You've gotten thinner. Your face is more pointed. Your nose is the same. You said: My father is Negroid, I'm actually black, I have black blood, my nostrils aren't vertical, look, they're horizontal. And also this spot on your nostril, this little blood vessel that's burst, I remember this spot, the only defect in your face, it made me feel tender, it's still there, I can see it, but quietly, calmly, the only thing that makes me feel tender now is remembering that it used to make me feel tender, but the little spot no longer makes me feel tender. You are far away, all of a sudden. Before, you were the one who said you're so far away do you love me what are you thinking about? Now you're the one who's far away, there, that's how it is. Are you okay? you say to me. Yes. You're having fun? Yes. And what about Pablo? You want to talk about him? To tell you what, I ask you, what do you want me to say? I don't know, you reply, I don't know. That I'm not afraid anymore? That he doesn't want me to be someone else? That he likes me as I am? That if I took amphetamines, do you realize I was taking twelve a day, he'd see that, right away, because when I've drunk too much coffee he notices it, because when we met I was taking a lot of Xanax, all the time, like cashew nuts, and I stopped without really wanting to, without deciding to, just because I forgot, I forgot they were in my bag, in my pocket, I forgot I needed them, I didn't need them anymore, do you see, do you understand? You really want me to tell you that?

Okay, you say to me, with that clicking of the tongue you use when you feel guilty, so let's be friends, I'd like us to be friends, just friends, let's agree on that. Oh no, I reply, what does that mean to be friends when we've loved each other so much, that change doesn't exist, it's even immoral to go from that to this, it's out of the question. You don't agree, you argue, you say Paula and her exes, she sees them all the time, I want to reply that she can't do otherwise, she's slept with the entire planet, if she didn't see her exes again she wouldn't see anyone, but I just say to you that maybe she didn't love them all the way we loved each other, you say that's true, but I'm not just an acquaintance, I'm not someone you meet by chance with whom you go have a coffee, I'd kill for you, and I'd even kill myself for you. You say that, and you must have been moved, and that should have moved me, but it doesn't do anything to us, to either of us, because we both sense that it's like a text learned by heart, you don't believe your words, it's even incredible how smug you are when you say it, you say it in a flat voice, without accent, without any emphasis.

"No, of course you're not just an acquaintance."

"We should see each other more, I need to talk with you."

"About what?"

"I don't know, to talk with you, just to talk..."

"We're free, you told me we were free, well we're free not to have anything else to say to each other, I have nothing else to say to you."

"But I'm not dead!"

He made my heart bleed, then. He seemed so panicked, so pitiful, at this idea of him dead, but instead of reassuring him, I wanted to be mean, I don't know why, I get angry at myself when I think back on it, Granny always said people are so nice, we're the only ones who are mean: It wasn't true, of course, she was so kind, but mocking too, mischievous, and annoyed when people aren't up to snuff, when they're too ridiculous, I must have gotten that from her.

"Yes you are, you're dead."

"But no, it's me, it's me, Adrien!"

"No it isn't."

"Yes it is! I haven't changed, I haven't changed that much!"

"For me you have changed, since I used to love you and I don't anymore. I used to love you and the person I loved is dead."

"But it's not true you don't love me anymore, you can never completely stop loving someone! That's not possible!"

"Yes you can, I can."

The people at the table next to us have left, there's a girl there now, I must already have met her, she smiles at me, I don't return her smile, I don't give a damn, I'm sitting with you in this café where we've argued so many times, where we've made so many promises, where you squeezed my knee under the table when we hadn't even kissed each other yet, it was upstairs, on the second floor, the lady at the cash register remembers, she acts as if she doesn't, but I can see, she remembers and nothing remains of any of that.

I want to hold you in my arms, I hold you in my arms over the table, over your coffee and my beer, and yes, this time, I'm sad.

seventeen

I'm happy with my rug and my new desk. Pablo and I went looking for plants at the stands along the Seine and, on the way, we bought the rug and the desk. He has taste, Pablo. He's not like me, he has definite taste and I take advantage of that. It's great to live with someone who has taste, it makes everything easier, it makes things light, you know what you want, you go straight for it, it's as if you were adopted by life, all of a sudden.

We also almost adopted a dog, a cute mini-dog with big moist eyes, but I already have three cats and Pablo goes to the movies a lot and you can't take a dog to the movies. We bought some clay pots and fertilizer. We planted, propagated cuttings, did a ton of complex and difficult things, gestures I wasn't familiar with, that I've done only with him, new gestures, without any memories or ghosts, we sowed morning glories, summer and winter lavender, jasmine, four-leafed clover, if I know the names it's because of Louis, Dad's friend, he's the king of gardens, he knows all the names of all the plants, he's one of those people who have always understood that sort of thing, right away, as if it's the easiest thing in the world, when I was so sick, and I listened to him talk to the trees, it was a great comfort to me. Then we went to see a film. And when we came back, my cats had used the pots as a litterbox, they had dug up the roots and eaten the flowers, absolute carnage, proof that we might just as well have bought the dog.

With Adrien, that would have made him shout with rage. He would have thought that a good reason to shout and then start moaning, about life that was too complicated, too unfair, always against him. We shouted a little at the cats, for form's sake, and because it was funny to see them run and hide, all sheepish, as if they felt guilty, as if they understood, and then we went on to something else. With Pablo, we always go on to something else. Pablo tackles life head-on, everything is a struggle, everything is a challenge, the world is divided between people who are greedy for life and impotent people who spend their time taking care of their little ulcers of the soul. Reserve a place on the plane or in the bullring, buy a computer, call the electric company, read a script, write one, send a big fat seedy-looking director packing, say yes to another role that has something worth defending about it—that's how he talks—he does whatever he has to do, whenever he has to do it, without any excuses, without annoying other people. Pablo's not a show-off, my grandmother said, she liked him a lot. He doesn't pose, he plays, and playing, this is also what my grandmother said, is exactly the opposite of posing. He charges, head lowered. He's like a bull you have to divert sometimes from his target, because, sometimes, his target is the wall. I like that too, in him, this perpetual bullfight side, bull and toreador all in one person, he isn't afraid of himself, or of life, or of other people, or of hurting himself, or of everything that prevents me from moving forward. With him, the future is now. What counts is the race, that's what he always says: What poisons existence is thinking too much about the finish line, you'll have lots of time to think about it afterwards, when you've lost, or when you can't run anymore.

I love running with him. He has the energy of those people who know that time is precious but who don't get worked up about it either. He runs according to his heartbeats, but his heart changes rhythm all the time, without any warning, by surprise. I don't generally like surprises much. I prefer habits. But I adapt to his surprises. I adjust to his swerves. No time he says, we don't have time to feel sorrowful, no time to be sad or afraid, the danger is past, see, we barely escaped it but we got through, we just have time to love each other and kiss each other. When we go to sleep he kicks the cats, kisses me, asks where are we going, where are we going, in the morning he's forgotten what got said during the night, right away he's ready to fight, he bursts out laughing, immediately starts worrying about me, are you okay? do you want your contacts? And he gets up without hesitating or turning over, he's not running away, there's nothing to run away from, who cares about the past, all the past can do is keep going, and it keeps going. I might be out of breath before him, but at least I'll have run. Now he's my speed.

He calls me Chatchki, I don't know why or what it means, when I ask him he doesn't answer, he laughs, his lips curling up over his teeth, he laughs, and I laugh too. When we met he didn't have any money, neither did I because of the divorce and all the money Adrien said I owed him and that he demanded from me and I was lying low and I was sad we'd come to that point, that we just had that link left, he was sad too I think, but then why didn't he stop, why did he keep talking about it all the time? In any case we were broke, and Dad, thinking for once it was time I got by on my own a little, had also cut off my allowance. Don't spoil me, Dad, I'd say to him when I was little and he gave me too many gifts, toys to the ceiling, raids on the Agnès b. boutique, hold-ups at Fnac, and then when he brought me to a famous couturier friend of his to try on the most beautiful dresses in the world. Don't spoil me, that was my leitmotiv, because I was more sensible than he was and I knew that if you spoil children you end up dulling their desire. Well here we are. He got the message, as they say.

My father can't see time passing. He hasn't really grasped the fact that I'm not twelve anymore and the time for education is over. Louise, he told me, I've decided to stop spoiling you once and for all. He spoiled me one more time, I'll have to be honest, when, after the clinic, he bought me a super-membership to a super-pool. But that was the last time. And that's how Pablo, when he grasped how penniless we were, said: You know about pasta with tuna fish? I'll make you some pasta with tuna fish, you'll see it's delicious, you need pasta and tuna fish, or tuna fish and pasta, the rich don't know what they're missing. Then, when he'd earned some money, we made risotto with truffles, invited lots of friends over, bought some good wine. Poor people just have to be rich, he said, like me. But he didn't think that. Neither that poor people just had to be rich nor that he had become rich, and the best proof is that, the next month, he didn't have anything left and he took me to Melun on the commuter train to visit friends. That's how life is with him, it's sudden, you don't split hairs, you don't moan, you have better things to do, you do them. Life is movement, it's dance, it's going from hot to cold, without any transition, skipping over lukewarm. Life is sometimes hot and cold at the same time, but it's never lukewarm. Sometimes though I call Time Out, I have a stitch in my side, wait a little. He waits. Paws the ground. Stamps his feet. He does something else at the same time, but he waits. I'm no longer a little bear, thank God.

I was happy, at the pool. I was the only one, I think, who came on the subway, and who came every day. I swam, for a long time, caressed by the water, in a lukewarm pool, the water was soft, there was music on in the background, I didn't think about anything, I glided, I pounded the water, there, take that, kicks, punches,

I don't know who I was fighting against but I fought, for a long time, for hours, I came out exhausted, my hair discolored, almost green because of the chlorine, my eyes fried but in good health. Sometimes, in the pool, there were ladies with their hair carefully done, with jewels on, who moved their arms and legs around a little but who complained when I splashed them, I shouldn't exaggerate, just because you're in a pool doesn't mean you should agree to get wet, so I went to run on a treadmill, or climb a staircase that didn't go anywhere, I liked the idea, before I took twelve amphet-amines a day, now I was doing three hours of gym. I had to stop when I wanted to smoke too much. And, when I really wanted to smoke too much, I took a lux-urious shower, with soap samples, ointments, oils with caviar and bath towels so soft and white I think they don't wash them they throw them out.

One day I invited Mom, we stole six towels, in two weeks they became rough and grey, maybe because I still had the habit of washing everything in hot water, sheets jeans sweaters: Boil everything, scour everything, it's all so disgusting. Mom swam for ten minutes, then she settled down at the bar, made friends with a lady of indeterminate age, hair like a lamppost, nice, little laughs, little coughs, and together they inhaled eight beers. Mom was tired all the time, then. She said it was the pollution, she said Chernobyl, she said age work trace elements. She didn't know, I didn't know, the doctors didn't know, that it was her cancer, stage three, too late to eradicate the tumor, the whole breast had become a tumor.

I don't think Pablo knows about the emptiness inside me. Maybe he senses it, maybe that's why he insists so much, come on, come on, I want to bring you with me, into my world. Louise, do you like the countryside? I reply no, without thinking, because I don't know the countryside. That's okay he says, you'll see what you'll see, we're going to Arles, when, right now, this very instant, the present. I buy some boots, a raincoat, *The Brothers Karamazov*, an Aspivenin snake-bite kit, that's the idea I have of the countryside: mushroom-gathering, rain, mud, snakes, boredom. And then we're in the train, the landscape is dry, it looks like Morocco, I wonder why I bought boots for myself, but it doesn't matter, I like it, I like what I see through the window, I'm happy, I tell him so, he smiles, he takes me in his arms, I let him, I smile too.

The problem in this kind of thing is reeducation. It's learning how to love again, how to laugh, how to feel, how to go out, learning everything all over again, like a burn victim, or a paralytic, or the amnesiac from that

Hitchcock movie who had to reconstruct a memory. Now I know that the countryside is seeing bulls, horseriding, singing at the top of your lungs in a café. I know I like the countryside, finally, with Pablo. I know that life can also be taking a train, wearing a daffodil yellow sweater, eating at a kitchen table, snuggling up in the arms of a boy who says to me my darling, my Chatchki as I go to sleep. He wants us to buy a house in the Camargue, here, now, right away. He wants us to have a baby, here, now, immediately. I should be astonished or amazed, I'm neither astonished nor amazed. I search through the silence inside me, I listen, I knock on my chest, hey in there, hello, what effect does that have when a boy says to you I want a child with you, now, right away, immediately? Nothing, it's still empty, I'm not completely cured yet and so I say to him we'll see. We'll see what? We'll see. I know that tomorrow, or soon, he'll have stopped thinking about it; I know he wants things right away, more than anything, but when the instant is over it's over and I know you just have to wait. Except there I was mistaken: The next day he forgot about the house in the Camargue, but he didn't forget about the baby.

eighteen

A baby. He wants a baby. A baby with me. With me, an ex-woman, who doesn't wear dresses anymore, or lipstick, or pretty shoes, or necklaces, or bracelets, or girl accessories, with me who hasn't had her period for seven years, ever since the baby died inside me.

So then, are we ready? the doctor had said. I didn't reply, I smiled and, in my smile, he chose what he wanted to: He chose yes, I'm ready. But, at bottom, I didn't know at all. I wanted what Adrien wanted. The doctor gave me an injection in my belly, which began to swell up very quickly. In ten minutes, I had the belly of a woman who'd been pregnant for nine months. A belly ready to give birth, but to a dead child. In the rooms next to mine, baby cries, smells that were sickly, sharp, odors of milk and vomit.

It's a pretty little boy, the other doctor on the sonogram had said, the bastard. He knew we didn't want to know. He knew it had to remain abstract, medical, a formality, the way you remove a wart a beauty spot a cyst. It couldn't exist, it had to be nothing more than a wart, a beauty spot, a cyst, and he had the nerve to say to us, showing us the grey images on the screen, it's a pretty little boy. We weren't looking. We were looking at the ceiling. We weren't even looking at each other.

It was a pretty little boy, but we didn't want it. We're too young we said in one voice, his actually, I had just published a novel, I didn't think I was either too young or not too young, I was twenty, the same age Mom was when she was pregnant with me, they must have told her too she was too young, but she had kept me. Adrien didn't want a baby. Not yet. We have time, he said, we have time. Time for what? Time to stop loving each other, time to get separated, time to leave each other, time to make this baby with someone else, time to give him the name we'd chosen together. That's not the baby he wanted. It wasn't with me he wanted it. I wasn't yet a drug addict, there wasn't yet that emptiness inside me, that floating feeling. But still, it wasn't the right time.

The bastard held out to us a folder with the first photos of our baby, our baby who would never have any other photos, our baby who was going to be thrown into the trash. I thought I had destroyed those photos. I found them again, last year, just after Adrien left. He left with almost nothing, with a cat, the computer, his new sneakers. So I told the cleaning woman she could help herself and I called the Salvation Army to get rid of the rest, all the rest, my skirts, my wedding dress, the sofa, the TV set, the curtains, the wedding gifts but also his suits, his shoes, his books, his whole orderly well cared-for fucking mess that I had decided he didn't need anymore where he was, in his new life with the new woman of his idiot life. The Salvation Army left the photos.

The other doctor, not the bastard, the nice one since you'd have to be pretty nice to agree to perform an abortion on a nutcase five months pregnant who hadn't noticed there was anything wrong, gave me the injection in the belly, then the other one in the back that's called an epidural and that made me woozy. I cried a little, for form's sake. But it didn't hurt. I plunged into a weird state of torpor that lasted I don't know how long, twenty-four hours they told me, twenty-four hours in the life of this fucking stomach that, despite the injection, didn't want to deflate. I don't remember anything. I just remember the nurse who kept coming to examine my stomach with a severe look. And the noise of the doctor's footsteps who also came to see, every hour, if I had let go of my dead baby or not. And the voice of a woman in the room next door shouting I'm not dead, I'm not dead and then not one more word, not a sound. And that's why my last real memory is of those photos, and of us looking at the ceiling in the bastard's surgery.

For I had taken a long time to realize I was pregnant. I had gained weight. I took flat-stomach capsules, I did abdominal exercises, I thought I had big breasts, like Mom, the same breasts as Mom, I was proud of my new breasts, but still I thought I was a little fat in the stomach, more than before. I had to have some pictures taken for the publication of the book, I was squeezed into my clothes, I had completely round cheeks, like a child, I looked younger than my twenty years, it's good for the promo, the PR guy had said: And my enormous breasts, is that good for the promo? I joked.

I joked but I was still wondering if I was going to stay like that forever, if it was a definitive change, if it meant I had become a woman, or if it was something else, if it was even more serious than that. On one hand, I liked having become a woman: It was about time! But, on the other hand, it was weird: A woman doesn't have a little baby potbelly, Adrien said as he caressed my stomach, at night, in our bed, you're playing at being a femme fatale but you still have a baby potbelly, I didn't think he was wrong, and I didn't like the idea, it worried me.

I went to see an acupuncturist who put needles all over me after asking me if I had blood in my stools. What in my what? Oh, no. The next day, I was still a little fat. The acupuncture isn't working, I said. Then another doctor fastened a clip to my ear, with a sort of staple gun, it didn't even hurt, to subdue my bulimia. I'm not bulimic, I told him, a little compulsive maybe, but not bulimic. Yes, yes, that's 500 francs. Adrien loved my new breasts, but still I thought the whole situation was getting weirder and weirder and I went to see a hypnotist: You're not hungry, you feel relaxed, fatty foods and sweets disgust you, 600 francs. As I was leaving I bought myself a panini with cheese and a pain-au-chocolat: What a moron that hypnotist is, I thought, with my little potbelly that was sticking out of my T-shirt.

I went on a TV show, on Bernard Pivot's book show, I threw up in the makeup room. Everyone thought it was nerves, and as a result I did too, and that really got me nervous. Pivot asked me why I hadn't taken a pseudonym, since my father was also a writer. I said something like you can change your name if you're named Pivot, but you can't change your name if you're called Lévy (yes, you can say it, my name is Lévy) and, when the program was over, I ran to the bathroom to throw up again. It's still nerves, everyone said. Louise is anxious, Louise is emotional, that mean Pivot just upset her with his questions.

I felt tired, all the time, much more than usual, so I went to see an ordinary doctor. I'm tired and I've gained weight, I said, do you have an explanation? He said to me I saw you on TV, what you said about your name was strong, very strong, the community won't forget it, and he prescribed Isomeride for me, an appetite suppressant that suppressed my appetite, it worked well; and also Guronsan for fatigue that made me full of energy, I was happy with that too; and also herb teas with a diuretic effect, they tasted horrible but they were necessary, he said, for the treatment to be effective. I lost weight very quickly, all over, except for my belly and my breasts.

I went back to see him. He asked me if I was taking the pill. No, my fiancé can't have children. Is your fiancé Jewish? he asked me. I replied yes, but I don't see what that has to do with anything. He is Jewish and he can't have children, how is that possible? I don't know, he's the one that told me, he can't, that's all. And you, do you have normal periods? No, of course not, I've never had normal periods, they come when they like, sometimes every month, sometimes not. And now? Now not. For how long? I don't know, for a long time I think. You'll have to consult a gynecologist in that case. Why? Because if you're gaining weight like this, it might be a hormonal imbalance, he'll examine you, take a blood sample, and in any case you should always consult a gynecologist every six months. I said okay and I went to see an osteopath, who examined me for a long time while he dangled a pendulum over my stomach. I sense a deficiency in aminotransferase, he said to me. Okay, what do I have to do? Nothing, that'll be 700 francs.

I make an appointment, then, for the first time in three years, with my gynecologist. She lives in the same building as I do. I went to see her a lot, before, when I was a teenager, when I had anxiety attacks and when I didn't have any breasts: I was very thin, with glasses and bangs, I didn't have any breasts and boys didn't like me. She was nice. She didn't examine me. She reassured me: It's because you do a lot of dance, it's often like that with dancers. Yes but I'm not exactly at the Opéra de Paris either, I do dance the way people do knitting, it's just a hobby. Yes, but don't worry, I'm pretty sure it's the dance. I worried all the same, and then, when I was seventeen everything came at once: In a year I had my *bac*, my disgusting periods, and breasts, I was proud, as if I was the only girl in the high school to have them, I walked with my back arched, breasts thrust forward, finally boys liked me, and I met Adrien, and I left childhood, the nice cocoon of childhood, very happy, delighted, with all life before me, the beautiful life that was just beginning, full of innocent enthusiasm.

So I go back to see her, for the first time in three years, the nice gynecologist. This time she asks me to undress. Can I keep my T-shirt on? First I'll look at your breasts, and then you can put it back on. Oh my they're enormous, these breasts, she says to me. Yes, I'm happy, I reply, I must be blushing, and I put my T-shirt back on. She looks at me in a funny way. What, isn't it normal to be happy with them, I've come a long way! I'm going to examine you, she says as if she didn't hear me. I take off my skirt, my shoes, my panties, I sit down on the horrible chair, knees together, is she going to make me put my feet in the stirrups, will I have the courage not to cry, the last time she couldn't examine me, I was on the edge of a nervous breakdown, I was wriggling every which way, I was crying. But not this time. She doesn't say anything. She just looks at my belly. After five minutes, or rather it must have been less but it seems like five minutes to me, she asks me if I have a fiancé. Yes, we're getting married. Okay listen, I'm going to examine you this time but I don't really need to, I can tell you that you're pregnant, five months pregnant at a rough guess.

I let myself be examined without saying anything, holding my breath, terrorized. It's not possible, I say. Five months pregnant, without noticing it, it's true it's hardly possible, she replies, in my thirty-year career I've never seen that happen. No, I say in one breath, that's not what I mean, it's not possible because he always told me he was sterile. Well how does he know that? I don't know, but he knows it, it even makes him cry, sometimes. Well, he can stop crying, you'll be a mommy, he'll be the daddy, tell him to stop crying. It's not possible, I repeat as I get dressed, you don't understand, he's preparing for his teachers' exam, he's not going to be happy at all. It was true: When I tell him the news, he'll be happy he's not sterile, but he won't be happy at all with the prospect of having a child, in just four months.

The situation is complicated. On one hand, impossible to have a baby, the exam, the exam, the exam. But on the other, with five months gone by in the pregnancy, an abortion isn't possible either, even in Switzerland, even in England, even on the Moon, impossible, too late, absolutely forbidden, respect for life, criminal. So, after moving heaven and earth, I get an appointment with a doctor, friend of a friend of a friend of Adrien's mother. He says to me he understands perfectly, the exam and all that, not the right time, he accepts the idea of a therapeutic abortion. What does that mean, therapeutic? It's for incapable women, loonies, or for deformed fetuses. Oh, I say, it seemed to look all right, the fetus, in the photos. But I don't really have any choice anymore, and I don't insist. Adrien asks though if there are any risks, if we could still have another baby someday. Of course, of course. Good, we say. In that case, appointment in one week. Okay, thanks. No problem. Result, we didn't have a baby and Adrien failed the exam.

Since then, I take the pill every day. Every single day, even on the days when you're supposed to stop so you can have your period. I never stop, and for seven years I've stopped having my period. For seven years, every morning, before I put on my contacts, before I know what time it is, what day it is, who I am, where

I am, who's sleeping next to me, I take the pill and, that
way, I don't have the disgusting periods of disgusting
women who have babies and swelling breasts anymore.
He'd be seven years old, now. His name would be
Aurélien, and he'd be seven.

When I'm really irritable, and I often am, I say it's
my period, it's because of my period, as proudly as I
did when I was thirteen, when I let a package of ultra-
thin Kotex peek out of my schoolbag to make my
friends think that I too was a woman.

nineteen

We haven't known each other long. One month, maybe a little more. He keeps talking to me about *faena, muleta, descabello, lidia, mano a mano,* Dominguin and Ordonez, Christian Dedet and Jacques Durand. I pay attention to one word out of three, generally. I like the sound of his voice and the accent he uses when he talks about those things. When I'm not listening, I watch him, his darker pupils as if he had started secreting his own amphetamine, his angry jaw, his nose that starts trembling, it seems to me that he was already talking to me about the corrida on the boat. He was mimicking the bull, chest out, *Clockwork-Orange*-look, *toro! toro!* shaking his towel, yes, I'm sure of it now, on the boat he was talking to me about bullfighting.

One morning he wakes me up at the crack of dawn, gets down a little suitcase from the closet for me that I fill on auto-pilot, puts me into a taxi, and we're at Orly. What's happening? I want to ask him, where are we going? But I don't, I don't say anything, I'm much too afraid of offending him since it's obviously been carefully planned beforehand, I must not have been paying attention but it doesn't seem like a surprise, it seems like one of those things planned a long time ago so I act knowing and don't ask anything.

In the plane I read, dozing, *Coin Locker Babies*, a novel translated from the Japanese about child killers who decimate Tokyo with a rocket-launcher that Mom had raved to me about. It made me think of you, she said to me with the intense look she has when she talks about my infant years, when we both lived together. Why? Mystery. But oh well. I pretend to read and that keeps me busy. Pablo is finishing up *Memoirs of Hadrian*, much more fashionable. I'm a little jealous. I even suggest we trade, but shyly, without insisting, and, in any case, he doesn't consider it, later, later, he says, without looking at me, dog-earing practically every page. Two hours later, we've arrived and we set down our suitcases in Madrid, in a former brothel that's been transformed into a hotel, with mirrors on the ceiling and stucco columns. Then, five minutes later, not even time to take a little bath, we're obviously not there just to have fun, we jump back into a taxi and we're headed for the arenas.

Beauty of this Las Ventas neighborhood. Excitement of the people. Pablo is very agitated, almost moved, I can sense a continuous shiver that goes through him from the roots of his hair to the soles of his feet. I'll have to live up to this, I tell myself. I'll have to follow along, not disappoint him, let myself be carried away by the general euphoria, the dust, the sun. So I watch Pablo. I cling to him. I kiss his beard he's just started to grow, a blue vein throbbing on his temple, his hand. It shouldn't really be so difficult. I just have to manage to catch his shiver. I pray. I beg. I say to myself, thinking it should help me along a little, that he's handsome as a Hemingway hero. I wait. But nothing comes, nothing at all, I might just as well be in Paris, sitting in front of the TV, in my bed, or even in the plane reading *Coin Locker Babies*.

We go into a café teeming with people. Total excitement. Aficionados. Flamenco dancers and so on. What should I do? I keep asking myself. How can I get into the mood of things? As an experiment, I smile. Mimic excitement. Talk loudly like the people around me. I don't even know what I'm talking about anymore, nothing probably, since I'm too afraid of falling by the wayside, so I just let out exclamations, onomatopoeia, but very loudly, like the others, they all have shining eyes and since I'm afraid there's nothing in my own eyes I put on my sunglasses and try to think about fascinating, or beautiful, or sad things, things that have had an effect on me, that have marked me, quick, some terrifying memory, quick, a scene that'll make my eyes shine and put me in the same state these bull stories seem to put Pablo.

What comes to me, it could have been anything else but that's how things happen, is this image of my brother and me, in Cabonegro. We're little, two and eight probably, the adults are seated at table, it's hot out, I'm holding my brother on my knees on the edge of the kidney-shaped swimming pool, he's waving his hands and feet around, the water is soft, I say "zut zut" and it makes him burst out laughing, my little boy, my little brother, he's a young man now, he's the one who lectures me when I have an overdraft at the bank, he's the one who bawls me out and goes to see the banker, he's wildly successful with the girls, he's handsome as Solal and John Cassavetes, zut zut he says in turn, delighted, beating his little hands and his little baby feet, and then he falls into the water. I leap in, catch him, keep him above me with my arms stretched out, but I'm little too, I can't touch bottom, I'm not strong enough to hold him up and hold myself up at the same time, I try to get more air and he ends up with his head under the water, I bring him back to the surface and I start to sink, we'll both drown, we're three feet from the edge, the adults are thirty feet away, I can hear them laughing and talking and we're going to die from drowning, they must hear us, they must think we're playing, help, help I cry leaning on my brother who's wriggling like crazy and whose mouth is too full of water to cry, again I hold him over me trying to move forward but as I try to get more air I drink a huge mouthful of water.

That's what I'm thinking about, in the middle of the Madrid café full of people, flies, dust, shouts. And also of the Arab lady who didn't know how to swim either but who saved us. What was her name again? Who did she look like? She's the one I hear in the café. Maybe Spanish actually, sounds like Arabic. Does my brother remember the scene as I do? Why haven't we ever talked about it? Hey Louise! You okay, Louise? Pablo must have sensed I'm not all there with him. Yes I'm fine. Listen, I want you to meet Sebastian, he's a bullfighter, he fought last year in Arles, he got two ears, remember, I talked to you about him last week, my friend Sebastian. Yes, yes, is that you? Hello, bravo, *cabonegro*, no I mean bravo. How can he not tell I'm faking it? In the café, on the square, there's a brass band playing, deafening, painful, even with my usual cotton earplugs.

Tres pastis, Pablo says, tres! I've never drunk pastis in my life. I've been drugged up to my ears, I've willingly ingested the most horrible garbage available to a human at the end of the 20th century, but I have my principles, I've never touched alcohol, I've always thought that drinking alcohol was, for a former child, the most extreme transgression and so I'm not familiar with the taste of pastis. So I'm happy to experience it. Madrid. Pastis. I taste it. I drink my glass in one swallow. I think it's good, actually. And since Pablo is calmly sipping his and putting it down after each swallow, I take his and drink it down too. Are you afraid? he asks me, seeing my hands trembling. Don't be afraid. It's amazing, but it's not frightening. Of course, I tell myself, of course, I'll tell him yes, yes I'm dying of fear, what a good thing fear is, it allows you not to be excited and to be quiet, it's the perfect alibi for a girl like me who is impervious to everything that's happening around her. I'm dying of fear, I say to Pablo. And I cling to him again. And he squeezes me hard. And I love him so much for squeezing me like that hard against him.

People are beginning to tango around us, probably because they're drunk. But things are also beginning to tango and spin, and suddenly I realize I'm the one who must be drunk. The buzz of alcohol in my ears. The impression of moving through the crowd like an over-loaded boat on a rough sea. I want to laugh, all of a sudden. It would be good to start laughing. He'd say: Great, Louise is happy, I'm so happy that Louise is having fun in a *feria*. But no. I shouldn't bother to now since I'm officially afraid and it's just as interesting to be really afraid as it is to really laugh. There's just this yellow fog in front of my eyes.

For the closer we get to the arenas the hotter it gets. In the café it must also have been hot. But I didn't commit a gaffe. I was too busy mimicking expectation and fear. So now, this sensation of heat: It's not an emotion yet, a feeling, but it's something, so it's progress. I keep Pablo's hand clutched in my own. We circle around in the crowd, on the beaten earth, amidst the manure, the bellowing. We circle around, but not in the same direction as the others, since Pablo knows a shortcut and, my fingers interlaced with Pablo's, I let myself be pulled along, against the current and at full speed, in the teeming crowd, smell of alcohol on people's breath, smell of ordure and waffles. With Pablo, you don't dawdle. You're not there to dawdle, or to take things as they come or go with the flow. So I walk. I let myself be guided and I walk. And, at the end of a long sloping hallway where we are alone, strangely alone, I can make out a narrow shaft of light, and the slow wreaths of dust at the end.

Pablo slows down, lets go of my hand, I take his again, he smiles, pushes me in front of him, our fingers still interlaced, towards the shaft of light. It's when we arrive that I understand everything. It's when I enter the cone of luminosity that I understand the excitement and the fear, I understand Pablo, I understand all the stories he told me to describe what I was going to experience. There are thousands of people here, and the sun, and the dust, and the music, and the heat. There's an open-air beehive, immense, noisy, smelly. And then I understand that I haven't understood anything at all, for never would I have expected to see what I see next.

I don't know what I was expecting. Nothing special, probably. I was probably just not prepared. But he did tell me about it. He did explain the passes, the *veronicas*, the *faena*, the *muleta*, the bull rushing at the horse, that's normal. He must have explained the armor on the horse, the cracks in the armor, the wild race in the sand. But I must not have been listening or understanding. And the instant I see, I start shouting: The thousands of people around me are silent, concentrated, but I'm shouting, I don't know, I'm not prepared, good God he explained everything to me though, I should have listened to him, but even if I had listened everything is going too quickly, I don't even have time to decide not to look, I stay magnetized, glued, hypnotized to the spot, and when the bull collapses I shout in its place and I collapse too.

Pablo rushes towards me, holds me up by the shoulders to keep me from falling, drags me, I don't know how, into the long dark corridor. I can hardly breathe. I'm ashamed, so ashamed, I want to disappear, burrow underground, shame, shame, shame. I'm so sorry Chatchki, he says to me, I'm so sorry, it must have been too theoretical, too literary, maybe I didn't talk to you about death. It's my mistake, I hid death from you.

twenty

I found a new gynecologist. The kind one, the one who lived above me when I was little and who diagnosed my five months' pregnancy, left for the United States. So lots of well-intentioned people, girlfriends, friends of friends, recommended others to me, every one better than the next, it's crazy how people love to stick you with their dentist or their doctor. I saw nice ones, serious ones, uninhibited ones, Buddhists, artists, homosexuals, old ones because they're better, young ones because they're more fun, kundalini practitioners, gyno-rheumatoid-psycho-homeopaths. But it was when I went out to buy some cigarettes, on the corner of the Rue des Ciseaux, that I saw the brass nameplate that made up my mind. Ring ring... Can you, by any chance... No, no emergency... Haven't seen anyone for seven years, so I can wait one or two weeks... Right away? Okay, right away, sure why not... I try to steel myself. I explain everything to the doctor. She's neither young nor old, neither friendly nor hostile, isn't scandalized or shocked or offhand, she intimidates me a little, but just enough so that I don't run away when she tells me to get undressed. The pill continuously for seven years? That's not very serious. Eighty cigarettes a day? That's too much, but that's not too serious either. What should you do? At the end of the packet of pills you should stop, that's what all girls your age are doing, you just have to do the same thing, even if it doesn't come back right away. All the better I whisper. Sorry? I said all the better. Oh, but you have to know what you want. You're right, I say, it's not really serious, so I don't know yet what I really want. Get dressed, she says angrily. And since I've probably blushed very red, she softens: And your mother—I told her everything, I had to, I outlined the whole picture for her—are you taking good care of your mother, at least? I do what I can, I reply. Good, good, that's important, not just for her but for you, it will help you get better too, it's as important as having a baby is.

I know, I say hurriedly, I know, even if it annoys me
to think it, I hate this idea that my mother's sickness
can somehow help me. As I'm getting dressed I notice
I've misplaced my bra, where is it? Where is it?
Impossible to get my hands on it, it must have slipped
under the chair, or somewhere in a corner of the room,
but I don't dare tell her, I've said enough things like
that, I hurry, if I were wearing a dress this would have
gone faster, you can pull a dress on like a sweater, but
no, I have jeans, I have to lace up my sneakers. Outside
I breathe deeply, I feel free, almost happy—a baby?
Why did she talk to me about a baby? And why are all
the people in the street laughing as I go by? It isn't till
I get back to my office that I understand: My bra has
gotten twisted like ivy around my left thigh.

The only thing that moves me, Adrien, in all you've
told me and all that I know about your new life, isn't
Paula, or your son, or your whole baldness story, or
your newly acquired gestures, no, the only thing that
has any effect on me now is knowing that you got your
driver's license. I know it's stupid. It's meaningless. But
I try to picture you, it seems so funny to me, it's so
unlike you and yet I can still picture you so well, you
must drive too fast, doing something else at the same

time, one hand on the wheel, the other in the girl's hair, the rear-view mirror turned toward your own face so you can make sure you're still there, make sure everything's okay, that you're handsome, the car must roar, speed up, leap forward without your feeling any effort, if I were the girl next to you I'd sing to you, I'd play with your face as I always liked to do, raise one of your eyelids with my thumb, look at the result, start over with the other one, pull your lip down, press on your nostril, pinch your cheek, and burst out laughing, you used to let me do that, you'd let it be done again, your face beneath my fingers like modeling clay, you let yourself be manhandled, you knew that even when you were making faces I loved you, you knew that even with your nose sideways, your lip up on your nose, one eye lower than the other, I'd love you madly and forever, it didn't bother you, it amused you, you'd say to me watch out though when I'm driving, no one drives better than me, that's true but you shouldn't tempt fate, I'd stop for five minutes, then start over, we'd laugh, I can imagine your laughing child profile, the red mark on your nose, your lips stretched out by a laugh that doesn't stop, your face bobbing as if mounted on a spring, I imagine all that, I would have liked all that, and also the open windows, and the wind puffing out your shirt, and our eyes blurred from the speed, I'd have the road map on my knees, it would fly away, I've never been able to read road maps anyway, maybe I'd have learned, maybe not, it's that way, no, it's that way, oh no, let's go this way instead, I'd have ended up chucking the map out the window and you, to get revenge, like the day you threw out of our seventh-floor bedroom window all your records of that singer I thought was cute and you were jealous of, you would have let up on the accelerator for a second and crushed my pack of cigarettes, you see, Adrien darling, I can't manage to imagine us any other way than squabbling like children, we were children, maybe that's why it's good, finally, that you left.

You came in your car, actually, and you offered to take me out for a ride. First I say yes, out of politeness, out of habit, because I don't want to hurt you either. Then, right afterwards, I refuse—being driven by you, now that we no longer love each other, now that we just kiss each other on each cheek to say hello and goodbye, no, no, I don't want that, it would be too sad, too pitiful, so I invent an excuse, any excuse, I say I have to stay home, I'm waiting for some people, I told them before that I'd wait for them here, you understand, next time maybe, thank you, thank you, it was good to see you again, good to talk with you again, good you wanted to keep me company. You don't say anything. You know there won't be a next time and that your driving me is a memory we'll miss, a stillborn memory like the baby, it's completely precise but at the same time it didn't take place, can you be nostalgic for something that never existed? This crushed feeling, then, all night long. As if you had driven over me, with your stupid car and your stupid driver's license. As if you had squashed me, like the pack of cigarettes from our memory that didn't exist, or like a cigarette stub. You used to scold me, remember, for not knowing how to stub out my butts. For years you tried to teach me. Look, it's easy, you start with this little twisting motion, to separate the lit end from the rest, and then afterwards you crush it down, like this, look. I never managed it, somehow. I still can't manage it. I'd let the cigarette burn out by itself, and that exasperated you, and I'd say jokingly someday you'll leave me because you'll be sick of the way I let my cigarette butts burn themselves out. Maybe you did leave me for that, after all. We were unfaithful to each other, and we admitted it. I took drugs, and we fought. I read your diaries, and you photocopied mine. I almost threw the cat out the window, you broke the bathroom door with your shoulder because I had locked myself up in it and was playing dead and not answering. I gashed my foot when I kicked a mirror, I locked myself into a closet, I overdosed on sleeping pills, I almost ruined your career, we've had sordid arguments over money, we've killed our future baby, and still we survived all that, and we told each other if our love has survived and triumphed over all these horrors, it's because it's indestructible. Well then. There are two things it hasn't survived. My way of crushing my cigarette butts and the way the new woman of your life had of botching up our life. She's a mean one, your Paula. I told you, that day, in the café. I even told you she's a bitch, a real trouble-maker, someone who shits in the fan to see what effect it'll have. You should have slapped me when I said that, or protested, or gotten annoyed, but no, you just tried to explain, you were offended, but just barely, no, no, you're wrong, she's good, generous, she has a lofty soul. Give me a break! A real slut! Someone who'll end up with her skin all pockmarked like Mme. de Merteuil in *Dangerous Liaisons*! That's what I told you, you didn't tell me to shut up, and that's what shocked me the most.

Yes, maybe it's better like this, in the end. Maybe we had to leave each other in order to become adults. Maybe that was the only way to grow up before getting old, not to become old spoiled babies someday. Maybe we needed that to find out one day what loving someone really means. Loving doesn't mean being the same, acting like two twins, thinking you're inseparable. Loving isn't being afraid of leaving each other or no longer loving each other. To love someone is to accept falling, all alone, and getting back up, all alone, I didn't know what it meant to love, I think I know a little more about it now. I look at Pablo, his half-closed eyelids, the sweat dripping on his forehead that the sun dries halfway down, the clearly defined shadow of his hand on the sand, and the hole of sky over him. He's sleeping. We left like that, on a whim; for my birthday, he gave me a big map of the world, and said choose: I closed my eyes, let my finger wander over the paper, and come to rest over Brazil. I don't know what we'd have done if it had stopped over Melun. Start over, he'd have said. Start over. At the airport in Bahia, our suitcases got stolen. No more clothes, no more swimsuits, no more books, nothing. Nothing but him and me in this hotel room, and the blinding white of the sea in front of us. We're happy.

It had started strangely, though: The catamaran reddened by rust pitched in the storm, and while the Brazilians, the tourists, the children in rain slickers were tossed about, vomiting from one end of the deck to the other, while a little bracelet-seller knotted a Virgin Mary around my wrist and asked me to make a wish, while Pablo stared at an invisible point on the horizon, holding on to his side, while I was concentrating so as not to be overcome by seasickness, I was wondering if I'd get an operation for myopia, so I could see far away, like other people, and not just two inches in front of me, nose to nose when I look at myself in the mirror, without my contacts, I have to come so close my nose is glued to the reflection of my nose. I'm squinting then. I can't see anything but my own nose all twisted to the side since I fell off the bike. I was saying to myself maybe I should also have my nose operated on, like Terminator-Paula, no, I'm joking, I like my twisted nose, Adrien was with his mother in Israel, we called each other up ten times a day, I love you, me too, no I do, no I do, but that's not mutually exclusive, it's true we loved each other madly, we were two children madly in love, yuck, all that smarmy rhetoric, all those pitiful grand sentiments, when I hear people say to each other I love you I want to hit them,

Pablo wants to hit women who wear hats, I don't know why, he doesn't either, he's just a little batty, that amuses me, we called each other up ten times a day just to say we loved each other, to remind each other of it, like the call of the muezzin, don't forget Allah is great, Allah is great, no, no, I won't forget, my grandparents presented me with the phone bill, 15,000 francs just to say and repeat that we loved each other, I was outraged that they dared to yell at me, I was stupid, I was egotistical, and I broke my nose falling off my bicycle, well done! I'll just have my eyes operated on, I just want to see, a little further away than my nose, maybe that's how real life begins.

I was thinking about all that, when it happened, that hot disgusting thing that came back, for the first time in seven years. The people on the catamaran had stopped vomiting, we could see the island of Morro in the distance, nestled in the sea like an animal, while a sticky tide of blood stretched out on the floor at my feet. I wanted to faint, to simulate a tetany fit, but I didn't do anything, I was paralyzed with shame, I let Pablo tie his jean jacket around my waist, clear the way for us through the crowd and guide me on auto-pilot to the Pousada das Flores. He put me down there, on the bed, and went to buy me a little green dress with white checks, in the only shop on the island. I like this dress. I'm wearing it today. It's hot out, dresses are nice when it's hot. I'm no longer an ex-woman. I think I'm happy. I even think I'm happier than I've ever been, even with Adrien when things were going well. It's true I wanted to die when we killed our child, but I don't miss it that much, in the end, this child we didn't have. I think you shouldn't miss the dead. All the less so when they haven't had time to be alive. It's true I wanted to die, too, when Adrien left, but I was never ditched before, that's why. I was always the one who left, before, when it didn't count. And it was still me who left, afterwards, when nothing mattered anymore. I know you can never break up easily. I know it's always horrible, and it always hurts horribly, and the one that's left always has the bad role, and always tends to say the assholes, those mean people, a nice girl like me, such a good boy, how could they have done that to us? But still, that's not so common, a guy who drops the woman he loves to have a baby with the fiancée of his beloved father. He wasn't forced to become this poor man's Hippolytus, was he? He wasn't forced to play the little bastard planting his little dagger in the back of the people who loved him most in the world. I remember one day in Porquerolles, my father had said to his father, what a pity, with all your talent, you haven't produced any body of work, and his father had replied, pointing proudly with his finger, I don't have any work because I have a masterpiece and my masterpiece is Adrien. What a waste! How sad! I think that day they were already lovers. She was sleeping with his father at night and Adrien would find her in the afternoon, the old caretaker had told me, in the master bedroom on the ground floor where he knew I never went because a bird had made its nest on a beam, and I'm afraid of birds. All that seems so far away, all of a sudden. It's like a pain that's dried up, patches of sorrow that have hardened, a great sigh that's been muffled, with just regret for all the nice things we still had to do and that now we'll never do: You'd need a crystal ball to guess the past. Watch out, don't be sad. Don't start crying again. If I start crying, I'll fall. And what would that mean, to fall in love, to fall sick? You can't fall a little bit. When I fall it's always from a long way up.

I'm sick of always watching out, though. I'm sick of myopia, of deafness, of silence. But I'm also sick of being locked up inside myself with all these feelings

I've forbidden myself, all these words I don't want to say anymore, it's better to die than say them I say to myself, into the trash with all secondhand pre-used words, it's like my heart, and my body, they're also secondhand, they've also loved, suffered, so what? I'm not going to be reincarnated, I'm not going to slip into someone else's soul, they're there, these words, in any case, they're in my head, in my throat, Pablo drinks them when he kisses me, he even hears them when I lock them up, what are you thinking, idiot? You really think I can't hear them, those words of love that you won't say? He's right, of course. I'm ashamed, and I'm ashamed of being ashamed. I'm ashamed of thinking them, the words, and even more ashamed of not being able to say them. I'm sick of this coldness inside me. Sick of not being able to be hot or sick anymore. Sick of putting life aside, and happiness, unhappiness, people, bullfights, death. Fuck fake life. Fuck darkness, silence, anesthesia, cats, jeans. Pablo's right. You can't stop living. You can't stop crying. You have to stop holding back tears, it'll give me cellulite in my face, after a while. You have to stop being afraid of being alive, he said to me the other day, at the airport. Every time you turn the radio up in the bathroom, I know you're going to piss. You have to stop, *Belle du*

Seigneur. You have to stop with your sublime love, beautiful perfect noble lovers. In the morning, we're crumpled, we have bad breath, that's how things are, you have to accept it, that's life too. Life is me leaving Pablo someday, or Pablo leaving me. I'll prefer someone else to him or he'll be sick of me, and it will be sad but it won't be tragic. And then the sadness will pass too, like happiness, like life, like the memories you forget in order to suffer less or that you mix up with other people's memories or with their lies. The insipid smell of coconut milk, our feet chafed by flip-flops, the immense centipedes running over the dirt paths, the crimson water of the Garapoa river, the little disheveled donkey that was braying in the puddles like a puppy, and this big yellow dog that's been following us ever since we got here: I already have memories with Pablo, that's something at least, it's like dawn breaking. You see, Louise, we're starting over, he said to me this morning. That's what counts, starting over. I don't love him the way I loved Adrien. I don't love him the way children love. Life is a rough draft, in the end. Every story is the rough draft of the next one, you cross out, you cross out, and when it's almost right and without any misprints, it's over, all that's left is to leave, that's why life is long. Nothing serious.